D0939967

THE SMILING HANGMAN

The town of King's Creek is in uproar. Young Matthew Lydell has been found guilty of murdering Janet Teasdale, daughter of a local banker. Lydell is to be hanged. But the town marshal has been delaying proceedings, and sent for a hangman from the county seat. The hangman arrives quietly, unnoticed. He tours the jail and the town, smiling, always smiling. What secret lies behind that smile, and what intentions does he have for the Colt riding on his hip . . . ?

OWEN G. IRONS

THE SMILING HANGMAN

Complete and Unabridged

LINFORD
Leicester

First published in Great Britain in 2015 by
Robert Hale Limited
London

First Linford Edition
published 2017
by arrangement with
Robert Hale
an imprint of
The Crowood Press
Wiltshire

A catalogue record for this book is available
from the British Library.

ISBN 978–1–4448–3522–9

Published by
F. A. Thorpe (Publishing)
Anstey, Leicestershire

Set by Words & Graphics Ltd.
Anstey, Leicestershire
Printed and bound in Great Britain by
T. J. International Ltd., Padstow, Cornwall

This book is printed on acid-free paper

1

Oh, the town of King's Creek was more than ready to hang young Nathan Lydell for the murder of pretty Janet Teasdale. They were eager, excited, in the mood for drinking, celebrating, and cheering when the trap dropped on his scaffold. The town figured that Lydell had had enough time to live as his twenty-first birthday approached. Yet here and there, knots of obviously angry men nursed violent urges that even the legal lynching of the murderer could not assuage.

That is, the mood of the town was difficult to gauge, seeming tangled and contradictory. Some of the citizens of the small town stood by or brooded in sullen resentment as if they held personal grudges against the young convicted killer.

Others, more determined to vent

their spleens, had become a little more aggressive. That is, they had already tried to rush the jail on three different occasions to yank Lydell out of his cell and do the hanging themselves. The executioner was too slow in arriving to suit them. This was an impatient sort of town, generally speaking. One thing that seemed to greatly disturb everyone in King's Creek was seeing a living, breathing man peering out a barred window after he should have been hanged and buried.

Oretheon Bean, the town marshal, had spoken to the more rash of these men quite firmly and had taken his pistol barrel to the skull of one of the ring-leaders, Randy Travis, who seemed to hold a personal grudge against Lydell, to make his position quite clear on matters. Travis understood after it was explained to him that way, but went away from the jail in a foul mood.

What it was, Bean thought, was that the men had had a large part of their financial lives taken from them when the King's Creek bank had been robbed a few days earlier, and if they couldn't do anything about that, they would damn sure force control over the rough order in the universe by taking care of things they could handle — like putting Nate Lydell where everyone knew he belonged.

Oretheon Bean wasn't much of a marshal perhaps, but he tried to do his best and he was as stubborn as they come.

'Boys,' he had told the would-be lynch mob, 'we had a fair trial. We had a verdict and a sentencing — all legal, the way things are supposed to be done, a credit to this town. Now we're going to finish this off the right way. No one's going to start a lynching, we're waiting for the hangman to arrive from Raton — because that's the legal way to do it. It's the man's job as executioner to finish the job and none of our own.'

'What, are you afraid to make a mistake and getting yourself in trouble, Bean?' Randy Travis called out — this was before Marshal Bean had cold-cocked Travis.

'I'm trying to keep this dingle-butt town from making a stupid mistake,' Bean said coldly. 'If you folks don't want me maintaining order, just vote me out next election. The whole bunch of you don't seem able to take care of yourselves. At least, you're not showing me that you are. Go home and put those guns away. If you don't take that well-meant advice, there'll be more than one dead man coming out of this.'

The mob moved away after muttering their unhappiness and Bean's deputy, a stringy man named Taffy, finally showed himself from inside the jail with a shotgun in hands.

'Well, you run them off,' Taffy commented as they stood on the dusty porch, watching the crowd saunter away toward the Belvedere Saloon. 'I thought for a minute there they might try breaking in here.'

'They'll be fuelling in the Belvedere for a while now. There'll be someone trying to stir them up again — Randy Travis, probably.'

'He don't like you much, does he, Bean?'

'Not much,' the marshal said, turning his head to spit.

'This will all be finished when that executioner gets here. They can't complain after he's done his work. Tell me, Marshal, where is that hangman you sent for, anyway? Shouldn't he be here by now?'

'It takes some time to travel from Raton, you know. Don't worry about the hangman,' Bean said as he stood on the jail house's porch, looking over his dusty, sun-shabby town, 'he'll be here.'

* * *

'It looks like Marshal Bean managed to chase the boys off again,' Sheila Porter said, peering out of the sheer white curtains which hung in the windows of Zebulon's Famous Restaurant. Clara Fine looked up at her sister waitress as she finished setting one of the round tables. Her eyes were troubled where Sheila's were amused.

'Why don't they just leave that poor boy alone? He's already scheduled to die.'

'This is an impatient town; always has been,' Sheila said.

'I know. You can tell late Friday nights,' Clara said with what was more of a sigh than a smile.

'Some folks — Nathan's friends and family, mostly, say that the town is just hanging him because they can't find those bank robbers to take their anger out on.'

'Who can tell?' Clara said, straightening up, stretching the small of her back. As she did so, she noticed the solitary stranger seated in the front corner of the restaurant near the harlequin window. 'Where'd he come from?'

'Who?' Sheila said, turning as well. Then, flustered, she began poking at her hair, searching for her order pad. 'How'd he sneak in here?'

'Don't know,' Clara said. In a calming voice, she told the flustered Sheila, 'I'll take care of him, whoever he is.'

And who was he? Clara Fine wondered, as she started that way. She glanced at the front door of the restaurant and saw that the tinkling bell alarm was still fixed in place. Both women had been working in the empty dining room, yet neither had heard him enter or cross to the table. The man moved softly when he moved, it seemed.

Clara Fine put on her best waitress smile and started toward the man in the corner. He was not from King's Creek, she knew. Where, then, had he come from? There had been no coaches that day, and the young, blond man should have been coated in fine trail dust if he had ridden across the open desert on that dry, dusty day.

He was not. He was wearing new clothes — all black she noticed — and these were if not immaculate, neatly brushed, and his hair was combed and slicked back — an uncommon sight in the dust bowl which was King's Creek.

And he was smiling!

You seldom saw a man smiling in King's Creek these days. It was a hard life they led out here, and recent events had just about eradicated the custom of humour from the town. Well, Clara thought, he was a stranger here, maybe that explained it. What it did not explain was why he was here. No one came to King's Creek without a reason.

'Sorry to have kept you waiting,' Clara said, her own poor smile still in place. A smile, she had been told, when she first entered the world of table-waiting, was sure to double your tips, especially from the men. Maybe so, but ninety per cent of her customers were men and they struggled terrifically against the very idea of tipping a waitress. Nevertheless, the smile continued as a habitual part of her working costume.

'It's all right,' the young man said. 'I

was finding it pleasant to watch you two working.'

What was that supposed to mean? No matter, Clara decided. The man who was not so young as she had thought at first, continued to smile, studying her with what she thought was too close a gaze.

'I'll eat whatever is handy,' the stranger said. I 'Anything that will fill my belly is fine.'

Clara lowered her order pad — that was a simple enough order to fill. The blond stranger leaned back slightly in his chair, hooked his thumbs into his belt, and asked pleasantly, 'What's your name?'

'Fiona Bacon,' she answered.

'No one's named Fiona Bacon,' the man answered.

'No? Well then, let me get you something on a plate.' Clara swished away. She was a little ashamed of herself for using her habitual brush-off on the smiling man. Maybe she would tell him her true name when she returned to the table. He didn't really seem like a wolf.

Rube Yates in his white shirt and apron was leaning across the order counter, big arms folded on it, when Clara reached him. She told the cook, 'A little bit of everything that's up, Rube. He's a hungry man who doesn't know what he wants.'

'All right,' Rube answered from behind a half-yawn. 'You serve him and get away,' he advised, rubbing his whiskered jaw with the back of his hand. Rube could be protective of 'his' girls, Clara and Sheila Porter. He would warn them when shady-looking men came in: gun-fighters, horse thieves and killers — Rube had an encyclopedic memory for the tough types.

Clara turned her back to Rube and looked back at the handsome, smiling stranger seated at the corner table.

'Why, Rube? What is the matter with him? Is he some outlaw on the run?'

'Worse,' Rube muttered, returning to work, 'Clara, that's the hangman.'

10

'Why, he can't be!' Clara said. She knew — thought she knew — what hangmen look like, big, stern-looking, draped in black, and . . . unsmiling.

'Well, he is. His name is Storm Hiller. The town constable pointed him out to me the last time I was down in Bloomfield.'

'I can hardly believe it,' Clara said, her eyes fixed on the blond man. Rube was rattling plates and frying pans around in the cooking area. 'I mean, he seems nice and polite, not like someone who's in the habit of bringing death to a town.'

'That's what he is,' Rube said, slapping a platter down on the serving counter. 'He can mean only trouble — to anyone who is near.'

Clara hefted the tray and started more tentatively back toward the table. She had second thoughts about telling the customer her real name. At present, it seemed prudent to maintain her distance from the hangman.

The stranger removed his elbows

from the table as Clara placed down the hot platter which held a sampling of beef, ham, yams and corn on the cob. He glanced up at her with bluish-green eyes which sparkled as he smiled. Somehow, Clara now found that smile irritating as if it were a part of his duplicitous makeup.

She did not return his smile as she worked. Clara also noticed as the customer opened his coat and tucked in his napkin that he was wearing a belt gun positioned near the front. She did not know a lot about handguns, only enough to know it was not one of those terrible large Colt .44s that half of the world seemed to wear in the West. Still, it looked deadly enough.

What did he need that for? To shoot the ones that wriggled free of the noose?

She knew she was not being fair. The hangman had as much right to wear a pistol as anyone else, and as much need for personal protection. She offered to refill his coffee cup and stepped back almost reflexively, as if the man carried some contagious disease.

'This is fine,' the smiling hangman told her. 'Thank you, Miss Fiona Bacon.'

After paying, Storm Hiller left the restaurant, using the back door as he had on entering. A slightly dazed Clara Fine watched him go; his visit had prompted conjecture, doubts and uncertainty in her mind. She found it hard to believe that the smiling man had come to their town for the express purpose of killing young Nate Lydell — and such an act taken not out of impulse, anger or hatred, but simply coldly performed for money. Some of the early diners had begun to arrive, and Clara was able to shake off her dark thoughts and lose herself in her work.

* * *

Storm Hiller made his way down the back alleys in the dusty silence of the evening. Few stars glittered, but there were enough to show his way. He had located the marshal's office earlier from the main street and thought he could find it again without difficulty. With his horse put away, his own stomach comfortably full, it was time he got down to business. He preferred to keep that business confidential.

Storm was not yet ready to face the inhabitants of the little town of King's Creek. The hamlet seethed with anger that could not be seen. It could nearly be scented in the lonesome night. Emptying out the bank had had the same effect as cutting its guts out. King's Creek was not done to death, but it was badly crippled.

Like a pack of nervous, uneasy dogs, the men of King's Creek needed to strike out at something, and their target had been presented to them less than two days after the bank robbery. Nate Lydell had gone out walking with young Janet Teasdale and only he had come back from their stroll. That immediately raised concern. Patrick

14

Teasdale, the girl's father, had been calling for a hanging before they had even completed their search, combing the pine and scrub oak forest lands surrounding the Teasdale ranch.

The girl's body had not been found; neither did Nate Lydell offer a convincing explanation of his movements. Nate seemed a little confused by events — many thought the boy was stunted, which somehow convinced people even more that he had committed the crime of murder. People conjured up all sorts of gruesome images in their minds and these flowed over into the jury pool. Patrick Teasdale, who had been yelling for the death penalty since the first hint of suspicion, was especially virulent. Randy Travis who claimed to be Janet's sweetheart, though no one could recall seeing them together before, anointed himself the head coyote in the mob and baited Marshal Bean at every opportunity. Also, twice Travis had gathered enough drunken King's Creek boys to threaten the jail.

There are those who might claim that public sentiment can't get an innocent man condemned, but in Lydell's case they were wrong. Assuming Lydell was, in fact, innocent. He had not protested when the judge sentenced him to be hanged, walking away meekly with Marshal Bean as folks threw rocks and spat at them.

Jocko Lydell was a different sort of man. Lydell's father was fashioned out of rough pioneer stock. He, on the opposite side of the legal spectrum, swore that he would remove his son from Bean's jail before a hanging could take place. Lydell had a fairly large spread as well, with ten loyal men working for him.

Which left Oretheon Bean in the unenviable position of having to guard his jail against Jocko Lydell's men who wished to free the boy, and Patrick Teasdale and Randy Travis who were planning a lynching.

Storm Hiller had been walking the alleyways, headed for the jail house and

16

pondering how little he knew of this case, when the long, crooked shadow of a man with a pistol in his hand stained the earth before him.

He stopped and the man with the gun stepped out of the shadows to meet him.

'I was wondering when you'd show your filthy face, hangman. Since I can't let you go about your business, I'm just going to go ahead and kill you now.'

2

The man's problem was that he wasn't bred to his task. He hesitated one second only, long enough for Storm, continuing along his way, to take two more strides until his body collided with that of the careless ambusher. Storm Hiller's shoulder hit the man high on his chest and the man with the gun staggered back even before Storm brought his knee up into the man's crotch. Storm grabbed the pistol from the man's hand as the lurking assailant released his grip on it to try taking care of more urgent matters.

It didn't work. The stranger threw up against the alley floor. He leaned forward, trying to catch his breath and ease the pain. He wasn't very successful at it.

Storm had backed away three steps and now held the man's own gun trained on him.

'You dirty bastard,' the stranger panted. He added a few other words, but none that Storm hadn't heard before.

'I'm just not fond of having men I don't even know wave their guns in my face,' Storm told him.

'I ought to have done more than that,' the man said, still puffing for air. 'Next time I'll finish the job. A man like you doesn't deserve to live.'

'Oh?' was Storm Hiller's only response as he rubbed at his ear. 'Here, I thought I was a fine fellow.'

'You know what you are?' the man snarled.

'Yes, I do. You're the one who's confused, it seems. Pick up your hat, mister. I was just on my way to the marshal's office. Now, you can come along with me.'

Hiller could make out the man's broad glowering face now. 'If I had my gun . . . ' he said menacingly.

'You had it,' Storm said with a shrug. 'Now I've got it. This is no time to keep making threats you can't back up. Turn around and start walking toward the marshal's office.'

He then cocked the inherited Colt for emphasis and the muttering man walked toward the head of the alley, moving gingerly.

They emerged nearly across the street from the marshal's office, and they continued in that direction, the stranger, having run out of novel curses, in silent dudgeon. The man paused as if waiting for instructions. Maybe he still had hopes that Storm would pat him on his shoulder, hand him back his gun and tell him to move along and play nice.

'Go right on in,' Storm said. 'Presumably Oretheon knows how to handle you local boys.'

The man had to knock on the door which had been barred, presumably against the swarms of night prowlers roaming King's Creek these days, After the third knock, they heard someone inside muttering and shuffling toward the door. It was cracked a few inches and Storm got a peek at a scrawny man in a red shirt, faded blue overalls, holding a Winchester rifle by the barrel.

'Who the blazes is it, Taffy?' they heard Oretheon Bean's voice boom out. Instead of replying, the man — Taffy — swung the door wider to admit them.

Oretheon Bean, his huge, waxed moustache splaying out from either side of his face, his thinning scalp freckled and red, sat behind his desk, checking off items on some sort of list.

'Storm!' Bean said, rising. 'You finally made it.' The marshal stepped forward and the two clasped hands. Bean was eyeing the man with Storm closely.

'What's this you brought me, Storm?'

'I don't know who he is. I figured you probably would. What he is, is a man who hides in the shadows in alleyways threatening to shoot passersby.'

'He did that, did he?' Bean said, making a sorrowful face. 'Jocko, I'm ashamed of you. You gave me your word.'

'Sorry.' The man whom Storm now

took to be Jocko Lydell, the father of the condemned man, looked briefly abashed. 'It wasn't nothing I planned, but when I seen this jasper strolling the alleys free and unconcerned, knowing what he had come to King's Creek for — I went a little crazy.' He looked at Bean. 'Are you going to lock me up?'

'Oh, you bet I am, Jocko. This man, whether you like his work or not, is a county officer. There's no excuse for what you've done.' He called to his deputy, 'Taffy, find lodging for Mr Lydell. I don't want him in with his son, though. That'd be doing him a kindness, and he deserves none.'

Jocko Lydell had fallen to a sullen silence and they watched as Taffy took the iron key ring from its peg on the wall and led him away along a dimly lit corridor. A moment later, there was a violent oath roared out in the voice Storm now could recognize as Jocko Lydell's, a brief scuffling and then the sound of an iron door slamming shut. Taffy reappeared shortly, his blond hair tousled, his hat in his hand.

'Man decided at the last second he didn't want to step in,' Taffy said, hanging the key ring on the wall. He wiped back his hair and reset his hat. 'I'm going over to Zebulon's for my supper. Want me to bring the kid a plate?'

'Bring them both one if you can manage it,' Bean replied.

'All right. Say, Oretheon, how long are we going to have old Jocko locked up?'

'Jocko's never given anyone any trouble around here before now, never bothered anyone before threatening Storm here tonight. I imagine we'll keep Jocko locked up until Mr Hiller has finished his business and gone.

'Tuck in your shirt, Taffy,' the marshal called out as Taffy started for the door. In the brief scuffle with Jocko Lydell it had been tugged free. Someone — Jocko Lydell — shouted from the back of the jail and Oretheon Bean, being used to such things, only glanced that way as Taffy exited.

'Now then,' Bean said when Taffy was gone. 'It's time we had ourselves a little talk — if you will close the door to the cells?'

Storm rose with a smile, crossed to the heavy plank door and drew it shut. He returned to sit on one of the wooden chairs which stood against the dirty yellow wall decorated with a map of New Mexico Territory, balanced his hat on a crossed knee and waited for Bean to begin.

'You probably know pretty much all I can tell you,' Bean said, flicking at a fly on his desk with a swatter.

'I got the brief sketch,' Storm said.

'Damn it, that's all I have, Storm! You know what's going on around this town, do you think I dare spend more than an hour or two out investigating? They've tried to crash this jail when I was here. With me gone, they'd be here in no time, grabbing Nathan Lydell.'

'Who do you mean, Oretheon?' Storm asked.

'Most of the town wants him, I'd say. A half of them, the kid's friends and men working for Jocko, believe the kid is innocent and want to free him; the other half are running with Randy Travis and Bert Crayne. These want to hang him and they want to do it themselves, maybe fearing a last minute commutation or a hangman with uncertain fingers. Mostly they just want to do it themselves, both bunches of them. This town isn't far removed from being a wide-open frontier town where a man does what he sees as right on his own.

'I'm having a hell of a time getting King's Creek to accept the idea of law and order.'

'I see,' Storm said with an understanding smile. 'I thought it must be something like that or you would never have sent for me,' he stifled a half-yawn. The long trail had taken something out of him.

Storm suggested, 'Why don't we start all over from the beginning? I might have missed something in your reports.'

Storm settled into one of the marshal's chairs, placing his handgun aside on a handy bookcase shelf. Bean glanced at the gun and commented, 'You don't see a lot of those.'

The pistol Bean was referring to was Storm's .32 calibre Moore/Smith & Wesson belt gun. Storm preferred to carry the less conspicuous weapon around town or when he was not expecting trouble.

'Let's have it, Oretheon — what else do I need to know about matters here?'

'What we've got here,' Bean said, leaning across his desk, clasping his hands together, 'is a rush to judgement atop an unsolvable crime. First things first, that would be the kid in there.' He slanted his head toward the jail cells beyond the plank doorway.

'Nathan Lydell, is that right?'

'It is,' Bean nodded. 'He was kind of sparking young Janet Teasdale. It was nothing more than puppy love so far as anyone could tell. Two kids who grew up nearby, Pat Teasdale having a little place abutting the Lydell ranch. That's the Corkscrew.' Oretheon leaned back for a minute in his sprung swivel chair, hands behind his head.

'The girl wasn't no more than eighteen, a cute little redhead. To Nate Lydell that would seem about the right age, and around the world most folks would agree.'

'Not the girl's father, of course.'

'No! To Patrick Teasdale she was still his little girl, would probably always be.' Bean sighed. 'That seems to be the way things have always been everywhere, too.'

'I suppose so,' Storm said. 'The kids always seem too young and they view their parents as very old indeed.'

'So that was all we had here, both fathers not about to give their blessing. Young Nate wasn't exactly welcome on the Teasdale property, but neither had Pat Teasdale outright banned him. Probably he was afraid if he did so that his daughter *would* do something crazy like running off with the boy.'

'What did happen?' Storm Hiller asked.

'The two went out walking one fine afternoon, and only Nate came back.'

'What did the boy say?'

'He just dummied up. I never got much more than a shrug out of him. I mean it was obvious he knew something, but what it was no one could guess.'

'But the jury took it as an admission of guilt?'

'Something like that.' Bean leaned forward again and said, 'You'd have to know the boy, Storm. I don't know if he's just not very bright or so darned shy — maybe both — but clamming up was not something unexpected. The lawyer trying him made a lot out of it. When Nate's attorney pointed out that they had never found the dead girl, he turned it around and made it seem like we had here one of the most cunning murderers the West has ever seen.

'And Nate Lydell, he sat in court like

he was unconcerned and wouldn't take the stand to defend himself.

'The town had had their bank robbed only two days before and nothing had come to light about who did it. They were damned if they were going to let this little fresh-faced rat get away with killing a young girl.'

'They must have been raising hell with you.'

'They still are; they've made it impossible for me to do my job. I can't leave the jail unguarded. So I can't ride out and see what I might be able to come up with concerning the bank robbers, I can't visit the assumed murder site to try to make something out of that.' Bean's eyes levelled on Storm Hiller. 'That's why I sent to Raton and asked for you. I'm in a bind here, Storm, and if things keep on as they are, neither crime will ever be solved.'

Storm had been thoughtful. He asked Bean, 'Is there any point in my talking to the boy?'

'Who can say? I haven't had any luck, but I'll tell you, Storm, the boy knows a lot more than he's telling — what — I couldn't say, but something did happen to keep Janet from returning home, I just don't know what and Nate, if he knows, just isn't saying.'

'Which seems to make no sense,' Storm said.

'Not to me! Considering the fact that remaining silent has left him standing in the shadow of a noose. But I suppose you'll be wanting to talk to him anyway,' Bean said.

'Yes, I don't expect it will do me much good, but I'd better.'

'Maybe just knowing that you're the man who's been sent to hang him will help nudge him toward reality.'

'There's always a chance, I guess. I just want to have a chance to see this young man. If he did not murder the girl, then he's covering something up. Something he'd rather die than reveal. Let's move on to the bank robbery, Oretheon. What do you know about that?'

Storm Hiller tilted back in his chair and waited, smiling. Bean was damned if he could see what was so amusing. Maybe, he thought, it was nothing to do with the situation, but just the contentment of a man happy within his own skin.

'All right,' Bean said, leaning back himself, 'what I know about it is as much as I know about the murder — which is to say, next to nothing. And I'm damn sure not going to find out anything else, pinned here in this office.' As if to emphasize that point, a barrage of thrown rocks could be heard outside against the wall, followed by incoherent jeering. Bean acted as if he had come to expect such disruptions and learned to ignore them, which was probably the truth of matters.

Storm Hiller refocused the marshal's thoughts.

'I take it that it was not your typical bank job with a few armed men brandishing pistols.'

'No — the bank teller, Colin Pierce,

reported for work early on Monday morning and found a few papers strewn around the bank floor, and the safe standing open . . . and empty.'

'Had it been forced — or blasted open?'

'There was no sign of it,' Bean said, rubbing a hand across his freckled scalp. 'Either it was a skilled jimmy-man or . . . '

'Or it was an inside job,' Storm said with a smile.

'Or that. And that seemed the more obvious of the two. But only Patrick Teasdale knew the combination. Not even his head teller was privy to it.'

'Teasdale . . . you mean the mur-dered girl's father is the town banker?' Storm's eyebrows drew together.

'That's it. A double blow to Pat Teasdale — if it was cruel luck and the two weren't related.'

'You cleared Teasdale himself?'

'He was in Sexton — do you know where that is? Fifty miles from here, in the company of a regular mob of witnesses — mostly the stolid business-type.'

'But you had suspicions still?'

'Of course! Anyone would. If only one man could open that safe you don't run around town questioning all the local drunks and hoboes. Then this murder business came up. Teasdale's daughter, Janet, was killed.'

'If they're related, I don't see how,' Storm said. 'Still, it's a possibility that should be looked at very closely.'

'Do you think I had the time for that?' Bean asked as if he were being accused of something. At that moment two shots were fired near the jail and something was shouted. Bean rose to his feet, then seated himself again. 'They just want me to go out and chase them. Figure they can slip inside, I think.

'I'm telling you, Storm, this has me going and coming. I'm almost afraid to make a move. I can't be everywhere at once.'

'No one can,' Storm Hiller said

softly. 'But you've got me here now. I'll give you all the help I can. We just need to have some sort of plan. The two keys to this mess seem to be Nate Lydell and Patrick Teasdale, wouldn't you say?'

Bean nodded silently, solemnly. 'Just try to get anything out of those two!'

'I intend to,' Storm replied. 'You know, I really had doubts about this assignment. I don't like disguises.' He shrugged. 'But Sheriff Drew pointed out quite firmly that it had worked once — down in Bloomfield — and it could work again in King's Creek. I have my doubts, but he's the boss, and here I am.'

'And I'm more than thankful that you are, Deputy Hiller . . . ' Bean's sentence broke off as the front door was eased open and then swung wide. Taffy entered with two trays of food, one stacked on top of the other. He gawked at Bean and Storm Hiller, hesitated as if he would have liked to ask a question, and then opened the door to the cells and went in.

'I guess tomorrow is soon enough to discuss the details,' Bean said in an overloud voice.

'I guess it is,' Storm agreed, rising. 'I haven't even seen your arrangements yet. Some refinements are almost always necessary.'

'I suppose they are,' Bean said, 'but that's your business and none of my own. I'll tell you what, Mr Hiller, instead of paying for a hotel, why don't you use my little house for the night? I sure won't be!'

Taffy had reappeared from the cell block where all was silent. 'Waste of good food,' they heard him mutter. 'Like trying to feed a dead man.'

Storm asked, 'Did Miss Fiona Bacon happen to prepare those trays?'

Taffy looked befuddled. Bean, who knew of the occasional ruse the waitress used to keep fresh cowboys at arms' length, told him, 'He means Clara Fine.'

'Then why don't he say so?' Taffy asked, a little frustrated still after his long walk and visit to the prisoners in their cells.

'He's still new to town, Taffy.'

'New come and soon gone,' Taffy said in a pinched voice.

'So we all can only hope,' Storm Hiller said. 'Especially me!' The man was smiling at Taffy as he nodded to Bean and exited the jail, Oretheon Bean giving him instructions on how to find his house as they went out.

That was a strange bird, Taffy thought as he collected his rifle and settled into his wooden chair, prepared for a long night's watch. How could a man whose job was death enjoy his work?

Maybe some did. Taffy decided that he would keep an eye on the merry executioner, for something was not right about a man in that line of work walking around with a smile on his face.

3

Storm Hiller made his way to the marshal's house through the falling darkness, guiding his black horse along the course described. The small white house was close to the centre of town, but secluded by a stand of live oak trees which surrounded it closely. He supposed the location suited the marshal well enough, being set far enough away to smother the night sounds from King's Creek's boisterous saloons, yet near enough to town that he could react on relatively short notice to any trouble there.

He stabled his horse in the neat little barn, found the key to the house in Bean's hiding place and entered the house, finding it small, tidy, close. Storm found and lit a lamp, which he intended only to show him the way to the bedroom. There was nothing more to be accomplished on this day, and he had spent long hours on the dusty trail to King's Creek.

In the morning he could . . . what exactly was he going to accomplish tomorrow?

He needed to talk to the prisoner, try to convince the kid to be a little more forthcoming. Oretheon had told him that Nate Lydell sat through his entire trial, virtually silent and expressionless. No wonder the jury had judged him guilty — he had acted as if he were. Then he meant to talk to the banker, Patrick Teasdale, who apparently had lost his community's savings and his daughter in the same week.

Were the two events connected? It seemed they must be, but Storm could not see how. Unless Janet Teasdale had somehow been involved in the robbery and then fled town. Bean had said that no one but Patrick Teasdale knew the combination, but people living in such proximity could inadvertently impart such information — a slip of paper in

Patrick's desk which Janet may have run across while dusting. Or a caution to her: 'If anything ever happens to me, Janet, at least you'll know where I keep this.'

There were a hundred ways, Storm thought, that the girl might have managed to find the safe's combination. Supposedly, she had been out walking with young Nate Lydell, but who knew if they had even gone anywhere? Nate was the only witness, and a silent witness is no witness at all. Maybe Janet had planned to run off with Nate, whom her father disapproved of, and share the money living the high life in some city. Maybe she had planned to dump Nate all along after he helped her with certain difficulties of the job which she could not handle alone. That could explain why Nate wouldn't speak up. If it was discovered that he was involved in the bank robbery, they would probably hang him anyway.

One thing was certain — they had not found the body of Janet Teasdale, which always in Storm's mind, left open the possibility that the murder had never occurred.

That was enough twisting and turning for his thoughts on this silent, cool night and after another minute of aimless reflection on a few of his back trails and one un-summoned recollection of Clara Fine's pretty, unsmiling face, he fell asleep.

★   ★   ★

The shots were as loud as cannon fire reverberating through Marshal Bean's small bedroom. Storm had rolled to one side, off the bed as the shots began — maybe before that. Some other small sound, the opening of a window, the cocking of a pistol hammer might have reached his unconscious mind seconds sooner, early enough to trigger a survival response which sent him rolling to the wooden floor of the bedroom as three, closely-spaced shots slammed into the plastered walls, filling the air with plaster dust and black, rolling gun smoke.

★   ★   ★

When Storm Hiller entered Marshal Bean's office the next morning, it was still early. The sun had risen not long before and there was still dew on the grass, a welcome coolness to the air. Bean, who had been sleeping uncomfortably in his office chair, opened his eyes. His face looked puffed and weary. His usually waxed and groomed moustache showed signs of neglect. Oretheon Bean thought that Storm looked different this morning, then he figured out what it was. In place of the little .32 belt gun he had been carrying the day before, he had strapped on his big Colt .44 in his tie-down black holster which now rode his leg easily. He was coatless, sporting a somehow fresh, white shirt.

'The boys around here already making you nervous?' Oretheon asked, nodding at the Colt.

'Some,' Storm answered with a smile. 'Let me tell you why.'

When Storm had finished telling the marshal about the night attack on him, Bean's already deep frown took on more weight. He rose from his chair and poured a cup of coffee for himself and Storm.

'How bad did they mess the place up?' Bean wanted to know.

'Depends on what you consider bad,' Storm answered. 'Broke your window glass, drew some grooves in your plaster and drilled a hole in your feather mattress. Who do you suppose they were after?'

'What do you mean?'

'I mean it was dark and I was sleeping in your bed.'

'Yes, but everyone in town knows that I haven't left the jail since this trouble started, so it had to be you who was the target, Storm.'

'Or someone who isn't from here and might not know that you've been sleeping in the jail. You have any enemies on your back trail, Oretheon?'

'Of course I do; I wear a badge. Mostly those people are either men with more mouth than gun skills or else they're locked up in prison.'

'Still . . . ' Storm took a thoughtful drink of coffee. 'I can't see how anyone would know that I was using your house last night?. Unless Taffy . . . ?' He looked a question at Bean.

'Taffy's not too bright, Storm, but he knows better than to talk about business outside of the office — besides, he never left the jail after you rode off.'

'Did you have any trouble here last night?' Storm asked.

'It was quiet for the most part. No one trying to knock down the door to get to my prisoner.' Oretheon Bean sighed heavily and added, 'For a change.'

'I see. Oretheon, I have to start somewhere so I'd like to talk to Nate Lydell this morning.'

'You don't believe he'll talk to you?'

'I guess not, but you never know, do you,' Storm said, 'unless you try.'

He slipped the Colt revolver from his holster, slid it on to the marshal's desk and waited for Bean to get the key to open the connecting door to the prisoners' cells. In the darkness of the corridor, Storm could see Jocko Lydell in the end cell, gripping the bars tightly, glowering at them.

'I've got a ranch to run, Bean! When are you going to let me out of here?'

'I told you — when you're no longer a menace to the public peace.'

'What about *him?*' Jocko said illogically. 'How many murders has he committed if you count them up? He's meaning to execute my boy right now!'

'He's not breaking any law, Jocko; that's the difference,' Bean said and then turned his back to Lydell, refusing to engage in further conversation with the distraught father of the condemned prisoner.

The heavy cell door was unlocked and Deputy Sheriff Storm Hiller stepped in, on to the flagstone floor to look at the wretch sheltering in the corner. Nathan Lydell didn't look exactly pathetic as he sat facing Storm on his wooden bunk. He didn't have that hopeless look that Storm had seen on men under similar circumstances, but there was a sadness about the young man, like a lost dog waiting for his master who would never come,

Lydell was a well-built kid with wide shoulders, but he was gaunt out from his time in jail and the worries he carried. Storm noticed that his tray from the night before still sat on the floor, the food barely touched.

He looked up at Storm, his eyes questioning. Sunlight was beginning to filter into the room through the high barred window.

'Who're you?' Nate asked in a voice neither challenging nor concerned, only vaguely curious. He watched with prison eyes as Storm sat on the opposite end of the plank bed, which was hung on chains from the wall. Storm answered him directly.

'I'm the executioner,' he said in a

sober tone, though a smile followed the pronouncement.

Nate Lydell twitched a little at the statement, and he made himself smaller at the end of the bed.

'Why're you here? Is it today then?' he asked, his voice quavering a little.

'Not today,' Storm said, still wearing a friendly smile. 'I'd rather not do it at all, you see, Nate. That's why I'm here — to give you a chance to tell me why you shouldn't be hanged for this crime.'

'I don't understand you.'

'It's like this — imagine this as a sort of new trial with only you and me present. I'll ask you a few questions and I want you to answer me honestly, as you might not have done before a jury.'

'I don't see the point in that.'

'Maybe there is none. Tell me first, where is Janet Teasdale's body? No one has been able to find her.'

'They never will,' Nate said with a surge of excitement. His hands were clenched together tightly, fingernails biting at his palms. Abruptly they loosened, and he muttered to the wall, 'They won't find her because she ain't dead.'

Storm frowned, tensed himself, and then regained his smile. 'She isn't?'

'No, sir, she isn't,' Nate Lydell said with ebbing forcefulness.

'Why didn't you tell them that in court?'

'Couldn't. There wasn't no point in it anyway, no more than there's a point in telling you.'

Storm only nodded. He wondered, was young Lydell denying the girl's death to free his own conscience of the crime, or was he telling the flat-out truth?

'Anything else you want to tell me?' Storm asked hopefully, 'anything else you can tell me.'

But Nathan Lydell had decided to clam up again. He now sat on the plank bunk, knees drawn up, arms looped around them, staring at the barred pattern of light cast across the stone floor of his cell.

After a few minutes of utter silence, Storm rose and said in a quiet voice, 'You know, I might be able to help you if you'd talk to me.'

There was no response so Storm turned to call to Oretheon Bean to let him out.

'Get anything from him?' Bean asked as he replaced the key ring on the wall and settled behind his desk.

'No, not really,' Storm said holstering his pistol again. He sagged on to a chair. 'There was one moment when I thought he might be about to tell something. He shut up again pretty fast. He kept insisting that Janet Teasdale isn't dead . . . '

'I've gotten an earful of that,' Bean said.

'I imagine. Anyway, I asked him why he didn't tell that to the judge and jury in court, and he told me it was because he *couldn't*. He covered his tracks up pretty well after that, but I caught the slip — he couldn't tell them that Jane Teasdale was alive. Why would that be?'

'I don't know, but if he doesn't open up pretty soon, it's a secret he'll be carrying to his grave.' Bean, who had taken the time to change shirts and wax his moustache again, asked, 'What do you plan on doing now, Storm?'

'The only logical thing,' Storm told him. 'I've got to talk to Patrick Teasdale and try to get a handle on his daughter's death as well as the bank robbery. Have you had any fresh thoughts about who might have tried to kill me — or you — at your house last night?'

'No, I haven't — with everyone in King's Creek against me, there's too many possibilities to consider.'

The front door opened to admit Taffy, returned from his morning rounds of King's Creek. Storm changed tack smoothly.

'I did see the scaffold in the back yard, Oretheon. I'm afraid the whole thing will have to be rebuilt according to specifications. In the standard drop which the territory has adopted, the drop has to be between four and six feet, and his height and weight have to be figured in so they have enough slack, but not too much for a clean drop and snap. We can't have the kid's head just popping off because of a miscalculation.'

'No, that's a little too gruesome for the ladies and kids who'll be watching the hanging,' Oretheon agreed.

'I assume that you have a properly boiled, oiled and pre-stretched rope as called for in county ordinances.'

'I'm not sure,' Oretheon answered, 'do we have such a thing, Taffy?'

'I don't know. What's the difference? Dead is dead.'

He then tramped out the front door again, muttering something about making his morning rounds.

After the door had banged shut heavily, Marshal Bean said. 'You've got this down pretty well, have you?'

'I talked to the official executioner in Santa Fe. He was a real bug on his craft. I just picked up a few points that would confuse the issue and delay a hanging.'

'We'll see if it works. Those that want the boy hung fast — Randy Travis, Bert Crayne and that bunch will be sore about any delay. I just hope it doesn't make them suspicious.'

'So do I,' Storm admitted. 'Just because this worked once before, doesn't mean it will in this case, but Sheriff John Drew, he's the sort that doesn't care to try out new ideas when the old one worked.'

'I suppose. But old John came through for me, and I'm grateful. I can't even wriggle around here. I can't find a single other man who is not firmly in one camp or the other on this Nathan Lydell business to take on as deputy. I'm stuck with only old Taffy.' He sighed and stretched his arms. 'I hated like hell to have to go to the county sheriff for help. It makes it look as if I can't run my own town by myself.' He looked down and away. 'I guess that's the truth, but I'm grateful to Sheriff Drew, Storm, for sending his best man up here to help me out.'

'We all have to work together,' Storm said with a smile, reaching for his hat. 'I'm going to get something to eat at Zebulon's, then I reckon I'll do some prowling about. We don't know much about either crime right now, and I'm not going to just shrug and walk away until we've shone some light on them.'

'Thanks, Storm. If you're going to Zebulon's — say hello to Fiona Bacon for me.'

Despite his grim mood, the marshal managed to smile and got a grin from Storm Hiller in return.

Outside it was bright and clear, showing promise of a hot day. King's Creek was slow in waking. There were a few shopkeepers sweeping the dirt from their porches, one heavy wagon trundling along the street with a load of copper ore, an early coach waiting for passengers. And the saloons which never closed.

Storm Hiller detoured past the

Belvedere just to have a look at the town's hot-bed of intrigue. There was a small knot of men standing on the porch near the front door, holding beer mugs. Storm had no idea who they were until one of the men, a shaggy bear of a man in a dirty sheepskin coat, grabbed a younger, slimmer man by the arm and turned him. He pointed directly at Storm.

'That's him, Randy! That's the hangman. Think we should have a talk with him?'

'There's nothing to say, except to tell him we don't need his services,' the younger man who Storm now took to be Randy Travis replied with a sort of muffled snicker. Then the two turned and led the small gathering back into the saloon. Storm continued on toward the Zebulon, his stomach urging him to speed.

Sheila Porter had just finished clearing off table number three and was passing Clara Fine on her way to the kitchen. She nudged the girl in passing.

'He's back again. Same table — your table,' Sheila said with a wicked little smile.

Almost in a panic, Clara looked around toward the far corner where Storm Hiller sat waiting for service. Again, he did not look menacing this morning. White shirt, dark pants, blond hair smoothed back. And that damnable, charming smile on his lips.

'You take the table, Sheila — please!'

'I'm busy if you hadn't noticed,' the older woman said, displaying the tray of dirty dishes and table waste she was carrying. 'Besides, don't you suppose there's a reason he took the same table this morning?' With a sly wink, Sheila hurried on toward the kitchen area.

Clara thought, oh well, it's not like he was one of those filthy, smelly buffalo hunters they had had tramp into the Zebulon a week or so ago. They hadn't tipped, either. She heard that after leaving the restaurant they had tried their hand at dismantling the Golden Concubine, one of King's Creek's smaller saloons.

With her working smile in place, Clara Fine approached Storm's table, noticing that he now wore a big Colt revolver on his hip. Maybe he just wanted to fit in with the rough men around the town. Maybe he was expecting trouble, which Clara believed he should.

'Good morning,' she said as cheerfully as she could manage.

'Good morning to you, Miss Bacon,' the smiling hangman answered.

'You know that's not actually my name,' Clara said.

'Yes, I do,' Storm replied. 'It's Clara Fine — a pleasant enough name. I don't know why you chose another.' He shrugged just slightly. 'But if you had decided to change it for whatever reason, I thought I should use the name of your choice — anything to please a lady.'

He delivered the little speech with just a touch of irony, a hint of mockery, wearing that damnably pleasant smile the entire time. Clara felt her feelings toward the waggish man slowly shifting — until she recalled with a sharp jolt that this was the one whose profession was snapping men's necks.

'What will you have?' she asked more sharply than she intended.

'Eggs, fried, hash brown potatoes and coffee,' he told her. Clara's hand trembled as she wrote down the simple order on the page in her pad she would hand to Rube Yates. Stupid! She told herself. Without looking at the smiling man again, she spun and walked to the order window.

The big cook, Rube, took the order sheet, looked at Clara oddly and asked, 'Something troubling you, Clara?'

'Me! No, of course not,' Clara Fine answered as if she had been caught stealing the silver. 'Why?'

Rube was not smiling, but his eyes were. 'Usually when one of you hands me an order, there's something written on it,' he said.

Clara grabbed the sheet of paper

back, stammered an apology and gave Rube the slip which had Storm's order scrawled on it.

Three local cowboys had come in, and Clara darted away with relief toward their familiar faces and worn jibes.

'What's with her?' Rube asked Sheila. Nodding after the scurrying Clara Fine.

'Her? Look in the far corner,' Sheila answered. Rube leaned out of the open order window far enough to see who Sheila meant.

'Oh,' the burly man grumbled, 'well at least he's employed.'

'That's the trouble,' Sheila said.

Clara returned to Storm Hiller's table with a full plate and mug of coffee. His eyes remained fixed on her while he ate, as if fascinated.

'Do you find me that interesting?' she asked in a snappish tone.

'I told you before — I just like watching you work.'

'I don't suppose I'd like watching you at work,' she said, summoning a gruesome image.

'No, I don't expect so.'

'Are you just going to sit here all day watching me?' Clara asked with growing impatience.

'No. Do you need this table? I suppose I'd better be leaving soon. I'm going to go for a little ride; would you like to come along?'

Storm knew what answer he'd get, and he got it. 'No,' Clara said, 'I have to keep on working, whether anyone's watching me or not.'

'Maybe another time,' Storm suggested with a smile.

The truth was that he was planning on taking a ride, but it would not be one that Clara would be welcome on. He meant to ride out to the Corkscrew Ranch and finally talk to Patrick Teasdale, whether he was brooding about the robbing of his bank, mourning his daughter's murder or not. Patrick Teasdale still seemed to Storm to be the pivotal man in King's Creek's woes.

Rising, he left some small silver coins on the table, waited for a minute to see if Clara might return, and finally went out into the sun bright streets of King's Creek. It was obvious now that the woman had heard who he was — or was supposed to be. He would like to have told her that he was playing a game of masquerade, but no matter how much he liked her, he knew that was reckless.

What now? Tugging his hat down against the sun glare, Storm decided to recover his black horse from the stable, briefly pretend to inspect the gallows they had constructed for Nate Lydell's hanging, then proceed to the Corkscrew. Before he had even stepped off the boardwalk he felt a nudge against his shoulder, and as he turned, saw a man staring accusingly into his eyes. What stranger would . . . ?

It was no stranger. The man's name was Handy Cooper, and he was no stranger because three years earlier, Deputy Sheriff Storm Hiller's posse had tracked Cooper and his gang of three to their hideout on the Rio Blanco, and after four hours and a lot of spent cartridges, managed to take Cooper into custody on a rustling charge which had stuck. Yes — Handy Cooper knew him and had undoubtedly been thinking about him daily over the past few years spent in prison.

Handy thought himself a fox with the women, sharp with playing cards and slick with a .44. Storm had to give him this last — the man was very good with a gun in a stand-up fight. He wore a closely cropped, dark moustache just now and was dressed in a dark brown town suit. There was a diamond ring on his little finger. Storm's biggest concern was that Handy Cooper would give away Storm's own game. But why should he? Was he even sure that it was Storm that he had just seen after three years?

Could Handy Cooper have been the man trying to shoot him as he lay in Marshal Bean's bed last night?

He was fairly sure that Handy would like nothing better than to see him dead, but Storm also thought the outlaw was perversely vain enough to want it done in the open, face to face, with no doubt about the outcome. There was nothing to be done about Cooper right now. He would tell Oretheon Bean that he had a potential lit stick of dynamite in his town, though what Bean could do about it as things now were in King's Creek was next to nothing.

Walking his black horse to the rear yard of the jail house, Storm found the two carpenters the town had hired to construct the scaffold resting on their heels in the shadow cast by their completed structure. The scent of fresh pine shavings filled the small, walled area. The men looked up with surprise as Storm walked toward them, leading his horse.

They were cousins, these builders, one heavy and slack with a rubbery mouth and beady eyes, the other older, narrower, going prematurely bald.

Storm removed a folding measuring stick from his pocket and walked directly to the scaffold, shaking his head as he went. Taking measurements, writing numbers down in a pocket notepad, Storm climbed up on to the scaffold, slipped off again, measured the drop, shook his head repeatedly and walked to where the carpenters, now standing, waited, eyeing him suspiciously.

'Anything the matter?' the heavier man asked.

'Almost everything,' Storm replied, tilting his black hat back. 'You're way off official specifications.'

'Nobody showed us no official specifications,' the big man said coolly.

'No? Well, I'll discuss this with you tomorrow. You might as well figure on tearing the whole thing down again. It's useless to me as it stands.' In a more sympathetic voice, Storm added, 'There's no point in working on it more today. I wouldn't want you boys to go without your due rest. You can check with me tomorrow in the marshal's office. In the meantime, plan on spending the day tearing it down to the ground.'

Neither man looked particularly upset, 'You the county hangman?' the bigger man asked. Storm said he was and the man only nodded. 'Then we'll do what the county wants. Don't make no difference to me and Timmy.' He shrugged. 'We get paid by the hour, and you've just made a little more work for us, and we can use it. One thing,' he said, scratching his great belly, 'we have to check with the marshal first, make sure you're the one officially in charge of this operation.'

'Do that, boys. My name's Hiller. I'll be back tomorrow. You should just pack up your tools and take the rest of the day off — at full pay.'

'That suits us fine, Mr Hiller. Whatever you want — you're the boss. Though I can't see why these folks running things are suddenly so particular. We've had two men stand on other gallows we've built — and they provided the intended result.'

With the carpenters on their way, pleased with the prospect of a day off, Storm continued on his way. He had made it to the middle of town, across from Zebulon's Famous Restaurant when the wild-eyed man appeared in his path.

The wild man screamed, 'You killed me; I'll kill you!'

4

The scrawny man was one of the strangest looking representatives of the human race Storm Hiller had ever encountered, and the man was mad as hell. The crazed scarecrow blocking Storm's progress carried his head cocked far to one side, nearly resting on his shoulder. The eye on that side was distended, angry and suspicious. One of his arms was wildly bent, resembling a chicken's wing. When he tried to lurch toward the mounted Storm Hiller, his step was tortured as if one of his hips was missing.

'Now I'll kill you!' the wretch bellowed. It emerged from his pinched chest as more of a harsh squeak, but the menace was conveyed. Briefly Storm thought he saw Clara Fine behind the window to Zebulon's, but he could not be sure. He had no idea how to handle the furious, disarranged man in front of him. There didn't seem to be any way of pacifying him.

From behind him, Storm heard a familiar voice shout out, 'Go home, Boy!'

Glancing that way, Storm saw Taffy, holding his rifle tightly. 'You're making trouble again, Boy,' Taffy said. 'Remember what happened the last time you made trouble?'

The deputy marshal came forward and with a sort of guttural snarl, the odd creature shuffled away, slapping Storm's black horse on the jaw, causing it to shy.

'Thanks,' Storm said to Taffy. 'I didn't have an idea what to do with him. Who is he?'

Taffy was still watching the man hobble on his way. 'That is Boy Coughlin,' Taffy answered. 'He used to be a feared man in this territory, if you don't recall the name.'

'No, I don't,' Storm was forced to admit. 'What happened?'

'He got drunk and went one step too far. Gunned down a local rancher in Farmington. Shot him in the back in front of his family.' Taffy turned his head and spat.

'I can't say I recall the incident. What did they do with him?'

'Why, they tried him for murder, found him guilty and hanged him!' Taffy answered.

'A short drop,' Storm said, borrowing the term from the hangman in Santa Fe who had coached him when he had first adopted this imposture.

'Well, that's in your line; I wouldn't know. All I know is that Boy came back alive, no matter that his neck had been broke, and they can't repeat the ceremony. Another of the ridiculous laws civilization has brought us. The law says he's legally dead, when you can see him right here, parading the streets and babbling.

'His mind was affected, as you might guess it would be. Someone must have tipped him off that you're a hangman,

Storm.' Taffy tipped back his hat and scratched at his thatch of corn-silk hair. 'He still has a grudge, but he don't remember it unless someone reminds him. He doesn't blame the judge, jury, himself, but only the hangman who came to execute him.'

'Is he dangerous?' Storm asked.

'Who knows? He probably rounded that corner there and forgot about you. He's far gone. Boy lives with a bunch of dogs behind the general store; we seldom see him out in broad daylight.'

'His condition's pretty bad,' Storm said, remembering his assumed role. 'They short-dropped him, sure. That's why it's important to have everything set up properly.'

'Yeah, I guess. The Platte cousins came by the office while I was still there. They wanted to know if you were actually in charge of their little project. Oretheon told them that whatever you say goes.'

'I'm afraid I had to tell them that they'll have to start all over.' Storm nodded in the direction Boy had taken and told Taffy, 'You can see why it's important to have things done correctly.'

'Yes, I can, thinking of it that way. The thing is, I don't think that Randy Travis and his boys over at the Belvedere will see it that way. They just want Nate Lydell strung up — and now.'

'I see . . . tell me, was Randy Travis ever actually Janet Teasdale's beau as he claims?'

'I've heard him saying that as well,' Taffy answered, 'but I think that was mostly wishful thinking on his part, I never saw the two of them together. It was always her and Nate Lydell.'

'What do you think actually happened there, Taffy?'

'Well, sir, Marshal Bean has sort of pounded it into my head that a lawman's got no right to an opinion. We're not judges or jurymen, what we do is what the law dictates and no more. Kind of like you, Hiller. Besides, our opinions wouldn't count for much, would they?'

'Not for much, no.'

'So, I don't have an opinion,' Taffy's voice lowered just a little, 'but if I did, I damn sure wouldn't believe that Nate Lydell could ever have killed that girl.'

Storm nodded, then asked, 'Have you seen Handy Cooper around this morning?'

'I don't know him on sight. Marshal Bean said that we might have a big gunfighter in town. Is that the man you mean?'

'It is,' Storm said heavily. Then he thanked Taffy again for handling Boy Coughlin for him and started on his way, still believing that he had seen Clara Fine looking out the window, wondering what she thought of his encounter with Boy Coughlin, and wondering why it should concern him at all what she thought.

★ ★ ★

The land south of King's Creek was mostly low, yellow-grass knolls with scattered live oak trees, although in the distance, through the shimmering heat waves, Storm could see a few higher rising hills with fringes of pine trees lining their crests. It wasn't bad-looking country, and he could see that in the spring with the grass long and green, it would be most agreeable to herds of free-ranging cattle.

This, as he understood things, was the Corkscrew, Jocko Lydell's ranch. The condemned man's father must have regarded it with pride often, and anticipated leaving it to his son, Nate, when the time came. Just now, Nate couldn't look forward to inheriting anything more than six feet of cold earth. Thinking that way, Storm could almost forgive Jocko's urge to kill him, but he thought that Marshal Bean had the right idea — holding Jocko in jail until after Storm had left town.

It was another mile on before Storm sighted the Corkscrew ranch house

71

which was of log and stone construction, obviously having been added on to at different times. There was no sign of activity around the house; Storm supposed there was a bunkhouse somewhere nearby, but could not spot it. He had been told that Corkscrew had over a dozen riders, all poised to break into the jail and pull Nate Lydell from the shadow of the noose. Did having Jocko locked up as well increase the risk of them launching a full-scale attack?

Now, here and there, Storm began to see cattle with the Corkscrew brand. It seemed an awkward brand to Storm, resembling two 'x's on top of each other. He began looking ahead now, anticipating the sight of the banker, Patrick Teasdale's house, which was supposed to abut the Corkscrew on the western edge of the range where a narrow creek flowed. He could see nothing. He did notice the shadowy figure weaving through the dusty pine trees farther up the slope, following him.

Who could that be? Any Corkscrew

hand, he supposed, with a natural curiosity about a stranger on their range. The thought of Handy Cooper flickered through his mind. He was still not sure if the gunman remembered him well enough to recognize him and blame Storm for his prison time. But Handy Cooper was dangerous enough to bear watching. Oddly, Storm also thought of Boy Coughlin, but he doubted that the man owned a horse or could even sit on one properly. Still Storm found himself in the uncomfortable position of being almost anyone's enemy around King's Creek. He wished that he had not adopted the hangman's guise again, but then of what use would he have been as just another man with a star in this situation?

Drawing his black horse to a halt in the shade of a small oak grove, Storm removed his hat, wiped his brow and made a determination. He would meet the man following him and find out what he wanted. That took less nerve than riding the empty land with a possible shooter on his heels mile after mile.

Storm turned his big black horse slightly upslope, passing behind a large, free-standing rock taller than a mounted man's head. He slipped out of the saddle and let the black walk on its way into the scattered pines. Clambering up on to a narrow ledge, he waited in the hot sun for the following man to appear.

When he did, Storm got a view of a well-built, clean-shaven man wearing jeans and a black shirt, mounted on a paint pony. The rider, whoever he was, did not look up to where Storm lay, but kept his eyes on the land ahead of him. Storm shifted his cocked Colt so that it was in a ready position. The man, passing directly below Storm, was halted by Hiller's voice.

'I think it's time we had a talk,' Storm said. 'Why don't you shed your guns before we make our introductions?'

The stranger reined in his pony easily and shed his sheathed rifle and then his handgun, looking up expectantly to

74

where Storm waited and watched.

'Kind of sneaky, aren't you?' the man on the paint pony said. Storm could see now that the man was young, in his twenties. His face was narrow and expressionless, his hands were steady and his dark eyes showed no guile.

'No more so than you,' Storm said with a short smile before sliding from the rock and walking up beside the man. 'You've been following me for a long way. What is it you want?'

Storm had already noted the pony's brand so it was no surprise when the man said, 'I work for Corkscrew. This is our range, if you hadn't known. I thought I'd better see what a stranger wanted way out here.'

Storm's black horse had wandered back. He rubbed noses with the pony and shook his head. Storm stepped easily into leather, keeping his Colt trained on the Corkscrew rider.

'Do you know who I am?' Storm asked.

'Yes. I'm pretty sure I do.'

'That puts you one up on me. Why don't we walk our ponies over to some shade and have a talk? You can leave your guns where they are for now — you won't be needing them.'

They swung down from their heated horses in the shade of a wide-spreading twin pine tree and seated themselves on the ground, not too near together, but close enough to speak. Storm continued to hold his pistol across his lap as he sat cross-legged, studying his man.

'If you're Corkscrew, you must know Nathan Lydell,' Storm said. A cool breeze had risen, ruffling the pines.

'I know him well, he's a good kid and a friend of mine.'

'Are there plans on Corkscrew to try breaking him out of jail?'

'There's all kinds of talk,' his hostage said with a shrug. 'There's bound to be.'

'Yes. Do the men know that Jocko Lydell has joined his son in jail?'

'I heard it, but no one knows if it's true or not.'

'It's true. I took him there myself,' Storm told the cowboy.

'You! But . . . '

'I have an odd antipathy towards men who try to shoot me down from the shadows,' Storm said with a smile.

'Is that what Jocko did?'

'It is.'

'Probably had some idea of helping Nate out.'

'Probably, but I didn't want to take a bullet to aid his noble quest.'

'No, I guess not.' The cowboy lifted his eyes to Storm's. 'You're kind of a funny bird, aren't you? What's your name, anyway?'

'I thought you knew. It's Storm Hiller.'

'Hiller — no, I haven't heard the name. You don't match my idea of a hangman. I'm Bobby Ryder,' the younger man said, offering a hand which Storm ignored, not knowing what Ryder had in mind. 'Mind telling me what you're doing out here instead of fashioning a hangman's knot or whatever it is you men do in your spare time?'

'I wanted to see both the Corkscrew and Teasdale place.'

'There's nobody at Teasdale's,' Bobby Ryder told him.

'I didn't think he'd go to work today.'

'He didn't. Pierce, his teller, will be conducting whatever business a bank does when they have no money. Teasdale is out with a couple of men looking for Janet.'

'He won't give up on that, will he?' Storm said. The trial was long over; hope of finding the girl faded.

'Would you, Mr Hiller?'

'No,' Storm replied. He supposed he would not give up looking for his dead daughter, no matter how long it took and how futile the hunt might seem.

Storm changed positions, stretching out on a bed of pine needles with his hand propping up his head. He asked Bobby Ryder, 'Is the girl actually dead, Bobby?'

Ryder started to speak, stopped and

then told Storm, 'Nate told me she wasn't and I have to believe him. He knows if anyone does.'

'He told me the same thing. The question is why didn't he insist on that at his trial?'

'Because there was no point in it. No one was going to believe him.'

'I suppose not,' Storm said. And he supposed there was no sense in riding on farther on this day — Patrick Teasdale was not at home and would be difficult to locate among this tangle of hills. If he could be found, he'd not wish to discuss the details of the bank robbery with a stranger. Not now. 'Does Teasdale have any of the Corkscrew crew out looking?'

'No, he asked for and got our help during the first few days. Everybody liked Janet as well as Nate. We rode out to help find her and also hoping we would not — as a means of maybe helping out Nate.'

'That accomplished nothing.'

'No. Then old Jocko . . . Mr Lydell

saw how things were shaping up as Teasdale against Nate, and he called a halt to it, saying we were 'giving aid and comfort to the enemy'.' Bobby Ryder smiled. 'The old man talks like that now and then,'

'I see,' Storm answered with a thoughtful smile. 'Surely Pat Teasdale isn't conducting his search by himself?'

'No, he's got a couple of men — I don't know if they volunteered or were hired for the job. Town riff-raff named Randy Travis and Bert Crayne.'

'I know who they are,' Storm said. 'Two of the main figures in the Belvedere Saloon mob that's so intent on lynching Nathan Lydell.'

'That's them. As near as I can figure, Travis is up here presenting himself as Janet's broken-hearted lover — which is a joke. I never saw Travis with Janet Teasdale any time, any place.'

'That's what I was told,' Storm replied.

Bobby Ryder was eyeing Storm closely. He had plucked a blade of grass and was splitting it with his thumbnails.

'You seem very interested in things — for a hangman,' Bobby finally said.

'Well, I want to know that I've got the right man swinging,' Storm answered with a smile.

'That's all I want,' Bobby said, 'and Nate Lydell is not the right man. But you — I thought the court determined for you who the right man was.'

'I like to dig a little deeper. So does Oretheon Bean, believe it or not.'

'I don't see Marshal Bean out beating the bushes,' Bobby said.

'No. How can he, Bobby? You men might be condemning the marshal for doing too little, but they've got him virtually forted up in his office so that he can barely step out the door.'

'I suppose they do,' Bobby admitted.

'Tell me,' Storm asked, 'what's your work load like around here just now?'

'I don't understand you. Do you mean are these heavy work days? The round-up is long over, Hiller, and the herds have been cut down. Right now we have to dream up extra chores just to keep ourselves busy on Corkscrew.'

'That was my guess.' Storm sat up, looked directly into Bobby Ryder's eyes and asked, 'I'm looking for a little help, Bobby. Would you consider working for me?'

Bobby Ryder blurted out a short, disparaging laugh. 'You mean to tell me you're wanting to hire a hangman's assistant?'

'In a manner of speaking,' Storm replied. He smiled and said, 'Let me tell you a story, Bobby. Then you can tell me what you think of my idea.'

5

'So what — you are actually is a deputy sheriff from down in Raton?' Bobby Ryder said uncertainly.

'Just like I told you.' Storm Hiller briefly flashed his badge again. 'Oretheon Bean contacted the sheriff for help. He had two major crimes he was supposed to be investigating but he's under siege in his own jail, unable to look into things.'

'But why the disguise?'

'What possible help could I be as an outside lawman also barricaded in the jail? Sheriff Drew and I used this particular tactic with good results down in Bloomfield once. He thought it might work again. At the very least I could delay Nate Lydell's hanging, and with any luck, come up with a new slant not only on Janet Teasdale's supposed murder, but also on the bank robbery.

And those two incidents are too closely spaced to be considered coincidental occurrences. At least in Sheriff Drew's mind. And in my own.'

'I don't see what you intend to do,' Bobby Ryder said, watching the smiling man closely.

'As much as I can as quickly as I can. That's why I need an assistant. I don't know my way around this country, and I don't know all of the people in town that I might wish to talk to. You, Bobby, certainly know this country and I assume you have at least a casual acquaintance with almost everyone in King's Creek. Having you with me can speed up my investigation. You know what happened and who was around.'

'I want to do anything I can to get Nate out of jail.'

'So do I, if he's innocent.'

'He is — I know the man. He couldn't do such a thing to Janet.'

'Even the deputy marshal agrees with you, and I suspect that Oretheon does as well. That puts us all on the same side.'

'Pretty much, I guess,' Bobby Ryder said dubiously. 'But I don't see what we can do — Marshal Bean won't want me anywhere near his jail. He knows I'd try breaking Nate out of there at the drop of a hat.'

'There's no reason for you to go into the jail. I will stop by and tell him I've deputized you, though,' Storm said. 'Then we've got some work to do. I'd like you to start thinking about what you know, what you might have heard about both of the incidents. I've a feeling they must be somehow related.'

'All right, I can do that. And, Hiller, if you're going into the jail house, would you tell Mr Lydell that I haven't deserted Corkscrew. And tell Nate that I haven't forgotten about him — I'm trying to help clear him.'

'I will,' Storm promised as they remounted, although he doubted that it would be much comfort to either of the jailed men.

They rode slowly down the hill, turning their horses' heads toward

85

King's Creek. Partway down the wooded slope, Bobby Ryder held up a hand, halting his own horse. He jabbed a finger toward the flats ahead, and looking that way Storm could see what Bobby had indicated. There was a great distance between them, but Storm thought he recognized the two mounted men riding toward the town.

'Isn't that Randy Travis and Bert Crayne?'

'It is. Either they got tired of searching or Teasdale sent them home,'

'I wonder why they're involved in this at all,' Storm said.

'Why? There's money in it, that's why. They can ride around in the hills for a while, pretending to be searching for Janet and draw enough money from Teasdale to support their drinking for another night.'

Storm nodded, he supposed that was all there was to it. He was getting overly suspicious, but that was what he was paid to do. What about Patrick Teasdale himself? Did he honestly believe that

Nate Lydell had killed his daughter, or was he using the episode to his own advantage?

Like drawing attention away from the robbery of his King's Creek bank?

'Do you know the bank teller, this Colin Pierce?'

'Sure, I know him. Not to talk to, but I know who he is.'

'What about him? Is he an honest man?' Storm asked.

'I'd say so,' Bobby answered. 'He's of the sort that stays honest because he's afraid of what would happen to him if he ever strayed.'

'Like that, is he?'

'He's not a man overly endowed with courage.'

'I'll have to talk to him anyway.'

'You're starting to think that talking with Patrick Teasdale won't profit you much, aren't you?'

'Yes, I am.'

'I have to agree with you,' Bobby Ryder said quietly. 'I don't think he's all that honest or that he's above telling a lie. There was an episode last year when we had three calves go missing . . . well, that hasn't got much to do with anything, does it?'

'No. Bobby, from what I've learned, Patrick Teasdale is supposed to be the only one who knew the combination to his bank safe. The marshal is sure it wasn't opened by some cracksman. So it could be that Colin Pierce had learned it, though he wasn't supposed to, just by working in the bank with Teasdale. It could also be that Janet Teasdale came by the combination at home — maybe written on a slip of paper left on the banker's desk. If she was desperate to run off with Nate Lydell, say . . . '

'Nate would never be a party to anything like that,' Bobby Ryder said strongly, 'nor would Janet Teasdale.'

Storm nodded. Then where was the girl? They had not located her either dead or alive, which left the routes to all sorts of conjecture open. If these ideas Storm had come up were both false, they led back to the first obvious conclusion — Patrick Teasdale had robbed his own bank. The thing was, Teasdale had a supposedly unassailable alibi, having been down in Sexton among a party of businessmen. Not that he couldn't have hired someone to do the job — like Randy Travers and Bert Crayne? However, it didn't seem that those two would be trustworthy enough for that kind of work.

No, Teasdale would not have trusted the money to anyone else. Therefore he must have somehow done it himself. Unless, despite Bobby Ryder's firm conviction, it had been Janet and Nate Lydell. But those two had been seen going out walking the next day . . . the day Janet had never come back.

If only Nate Lydell would speak up, but he had not at his trial and was unlikely to do so now, even as the hour of his death neared, personified by Storm Hiller.

'Who were the men Patrick Teasdale was meeting with down in Sexton?' Storm asked, his thoughts veering aside. They were near enough now to see King's Creek, a town loafing in late afternoon. No one could be seen along the streets.

'Well, Deputy — I'd better not call you that, had I? I'm hardly the man to ask; I'm not exactly in the same social group as those people. I did hear Jocko Lydell talking about them that day, calling them a bunch of over-stuffed snobs among other things.

'The banker from Sexton was going to be there and some of the high-rolling businessmen in this county. Dawson who runs the freight line, Dalton Short who is a railroad man, Buck Dewar who owns two of our local copper mines . . . I can't remember any more, though Lydell named some others. I took it that it was some sort of political rally, the kind where the bosses decide who's going to run our lives for the next few years. I never met any of them except for Short when we were having items shipped in for the new house once.'

'Quite an array of witnesses for Patrick Teasdale.'

'I'd say so. It couldn't have been any better unless he showed up with the Supreme Court.'

Topping the crest of the hill surrounding the valley where King's Creek was nestled, Storm asked Bobby, 'I'm going over to the marshal's office first, where can I meet you in an hour or so?'

'I'll be in Zebulon's. There's a little blonde woman there named Peony Cowper working there, who I sort of favour, though she seems to think a working cowboy is not quite in her social range, either.'

'Sort of a memorable name,' Storm said as they trailed their ponies along the dusty main street.

'Yes,' Bobby said, briefly removing his hat and scratching his head with the same hand. 'It kind of made me wonder if she was giving it to me straight. But then, there's another girl working there named Fiona Bacon, so you never know with names, do you?'

'I guess you don't,' Storm answered, holding back a smile. He had heard the blonde waitress working at Zebulon's called Sheila by the cook, but he didn't think it was his place to reveal 'Peony's' name to Bobby Ryder. Neither Clara Fine nor Sheila Porter thought it was a good idea to furnish their true names to every cowboy and drifter who came through Zebulon's. Probably they were right, who knew. Women always would have their secrets.

Storm Hiller swung down from his black horse in front of the marshal's office, and let Bobby Ryder continue along his way to Zebulon's Famous Restaurant, presumably to further explore the mystery of Peony Cowper. Storm knocked on the heavy door twice and waited. From the weight of the footsteps crossing the floor of the jail, Storm expected to see Oretheon Bean when the door was opened. Taffy would probably be out on his evening rounds.

He was not disappointed when the florid, somewhat forlorn face of the moustachioed marshal appeared in the door gap.

' 'Lo, Storm,' Bean said, opening the door wider.

The man sounded extremely weary. How long had it been since Bean had stretched out on a bed, untroubled by thoughts of gunfire and mayhem? We don't pay our lawmen enough and when they do what they've been hired to do, they only get criticism for their efforts, Storm thought. Somehow things get rapidly turned around so that yesterday's criminals are today's heroes. A lawman can only watch and bear it.

'I've got something I want you to look at, Storm,' Bean said, dropping the bar across the door. He led the way back to his desk. Storm took the wooden chair facing him and placed his hat, its brim damp with sweat, on the corner of the marshal's desk. Oretheon fingered a single piece of yellowish paper across the desk for Storm to read. The writing was at all angles, written in pencil, most of the letters poorly formed. The author's intent was clear, however. It read:

O, Bean. Will all be back. Have not given up on taking that girl-murdering scum away from you and ministering real justice by the neck. Don't try goon to sleep on us, marshal. We have dynamite and are intent using it to get our way — JUSTICE.

'Who wrote this?' Storm asked with concern.

'I don't know who in particular, but it has to be somebody liquered up in the Belvedere Saloon — Randy Travis is always my first guess.'

'Do they mean this? Do they even have access to dynamite?'

'Probably. Buck Dewar is running two copper mines up in the Stover Hills, you know.'

'I knew there was mining going on around here somewhere. I suppose it wouldn't take much for anybody with the right connections to come by some. But why, Oretheon? Don't they know that blowing the jail up could kill everyone inside, including the man they claim to want out?'

'It would save them the price of a rope,' Bean said dismally.

'It would also destroy half of this block of buildings. This was written by an insane man.'

'I don't think they're insane, Storm; they simply don't care about anybody else, anything but winning.'

That nearly enough fitted Storm's definition of insanity, but he didn't pursue it. 'Do you have any plans for preventing this?' he asked.

'I'll have Taffy on constant patrol outside in case they try to sneak up here. If they come in a crowd, I'll just have to shoot down the first man starting this way. Hell of a way to do business.'

'I'll be around,' Storm promised. 'I'll help you out the best I can, Oretheon. That's why I was sent here, remember?'

'I thank you for that, but we're still three men against maybe forty.'

'You could just let them have Nate Lydell — the kid's pretty much doomed anyway, isn't he?'

'Would you, Storm? Is that the way Sheriff Drew taught you to do things?'

'No, sir,' Storm said with a quick smile. 'That is no option at all.' Storm Hiller was silent for a few moments, then he told Oretheon Bean, 'I've taken on a deputy of my own. That might help our odds a little.'

'Where could you find a man?' Bean asked. 'I've been asking for men for a week now with no takers.'

'Do you know a cowboy named Bobby Ryder?'

'Yes, I know Bobby Ryder!' Bean said with controlled fury. 'He's one of those Corkscrew men determined to break young Lydell out of here.'

'Is Bobby here?' a weak voice from the jail cells called.

'No, he ain't here!' Bean bellowed back.

'I want to talk to him,' the same voice, recognizable now as Nate Lydell's, pleaded.

'He ain't here! He's not going to be

here,' Oretheon Bean shouted back in a slightly modulated voice.

Storm Hiller's smile was slight. 'That's pretty much the reaction Bobby expected; that's why I didn't bring him over with me.'

The marshal drummed his thick fingers on his desktop. 'You trust this man to work for you?'

'Until he gives me a reason not to,' Storm answered. 'It's not that easy for me to find a helper, either, you know?'

'All right,' Bean said, growling softly. 'You've done it, reported it, and he's your problem. Just don't bring him into my jail.'

'That's understood. Oretheon? Have you seen Handy Cooper around town?'

'I can't get around town myself,' was Bean's unhappy reply. 'Why do you ask?'

'He may be carrying a grudge against me. Though it could be that he's forgotten what I even look like by now — I hope so.'

'I told Taffy to keep an eye out for him. I'll remind him.'

'Thanks. I don't know what he's up to in King's Creek. It could be nothing at all except passing through. All these coincidences around here bother me, though.'

'You mean the bank robbery and Janet's supposed murder?'

'That's exactly what I mean. Did you have the opportunity to interview Colin Pierce at the bank?'

'Not what you'd really call an interview,' Bean reflected. 'He came running in here and reported that the bank had been robbed over the weekend. I asked him if he had any idea who had done it, and he told me no.'

'I think I'd better talk to him again.' Storm studied Bean's worried face. 'But I guess that can wait until tomorrow.' Someone had warned of an assault on the jail with explosives. That kind of threat could not be dismissed with a shrug. 'It's close to dark out there,' Storm added, peering through the narrow window cut in the oaken door. 'The streets are still quiet. You say that Taffy is outside?'

'That's right, keeping an eye on the back and the alleys.'

'Bobby and I will be back with rifles. We'll help him stand watch. If they come in a bunch he might not be able to keep them all off you by himself.'

'I'd appreciate it, Storm. Those men are getting pretty impatient about seeing the hanging done.'

'If they're waiting for me to do it, they're going to get a lot more impatient. The Platte cousins are showing up to work tomorrow with a load of sub-standard lumber for the gallows.'

'How can you be sure of that?' Bean asked.

'Oh, I am sure,' Storm said with a smile. 'We haven't even got the rope prepared yet. Have you had anyone stretching and oiling it?'

'No, I suppose the conditions around here have caused me to become downright negligent.'

'So it would seem.' Storm turned to

face the marshal again. 'I'm going over to Zebulon's to get something to eat. Then, as I told you, Bobby and I will be back to help with the night watch. We can't let this whole problem finish with a bang.'

'No,' Oretheon Bean agreed, 'though I've the feeling it might if those boys are as determined as they seem to be.'

Then, after a few minutes spent delivering Bobby Ryder's messages to Nathan and Jocko Lydell, Storm stepped outside into the slowly settling evening to make his way toward Zebulon's, wondering if Peony Cowper and Fiona Bacon were both working that night. Up the street, the Belvedere Saloon continued to blare and nearly to rumble with excitement as it filled up with the sundown crowd and gangs of would-be rioters, one of whom was sheltering a dynamite charge threatening to blow the top off any semblance of quiet peace the night had gathered about itself.

6

Storm's welcome at Zebulon's was about as he would have expected. Many morose faces looked up from their plates of food and fixed eyes in his direction, seeming to wish that he was the one they would soon see hanging on a gibbet instead of young Nate Lydell. The other half, or most of them, seemed to be wondering why the hangman was show- ing such hesitation in getting a job done that needed doing. There were very few who seemed indifferent to his presence.

He spotted Bobby Ryder at a table diagonally opposite from what had become Storm's regular spot by the front window. Bobby sat in a dark far corner, ceramic cup of coffee between both hands. Bobby's eyes lifted, recog- nized Storm and then shifted away. With the town as divided as it was, more than a few questions flitted through the eyes of the other customers as the hangman took a seat across the table from the Corkscrew cowhand.

'I thought I was getting hard looks from the Teasdale people before you got here,' Bobby said.

'The Belvedere Saloon people, you mean,' Storm pointed out.

Bobby shrugged. 'Yeah, maybe. Teasdale doesn't really have many friends, though Janet did.'

'Well . . . ' Storm started to speak but broke off as he recognized the blonde waitress approaching their table with a tin tray filled with Bobby's order. Bobby's eyes had softened at the sight of Sheila Porter; the girl's face, however, remained expressionless, nearly stony. She placed the plates down with negligent emphasis as Bobby's hound dog eyes followed her every movement.

Sheila tucked the empty tray under one arm and produced her ordering pad. 'What'll you have?' she asked Storm Hiller. 'Or aren't you ready to order?'

'Oh, I'm ready to order,' Storm answered with a friendly smile. 'But I couldn't get my regular table tonight, and I'd feel more comfortable with my regular waitress. Could you, maybe, tell Fiona Bacon that I'd like her to take my order?'

Sheila Porter pursed her lips tightly, showing exasperation and replied, 'I'll see,' before she walked stiffly away.

'You take some liberties,' Bobby said between bites of mashed potatoes, 'asking for your own waitress.'

'I do, don't I?' Storm agreed. Whatever minor consternation he might have caused Sheila was, he felt, justified by the sight of the perky Clara Fine, following Sheila's pointing finger across the room toward his table, hips and shoulders in natural rhythm, her mouth drawn tight, her eyes on everywhere but where he sat.

'Help you?' she asked shortly without actually snapping, It was Storm's turn to gawk as Bobby's turned down eyes grew more interested in his pork chops and mashed potatoes. Storm indulged himself, studying the woman's trim figure, her generous mouth and bright eyes, slightly curled, glossy dark hair.

'I'll have what he's having,' Storm said, trying his broadest smile on Clara Fine.

'You couldn't have told the other girl that?' Clara asked sharply.

'I could have, Clara,' Storm replied, 'but then I wouldn't have had the chance to see you again, would I?'

Clara Fine started to snap out a response, but after all, she was working; she was used to all kinds in this rough town and it was hard to produce an anger toward the gently smiling man. She turned sharply and strutted away.

'Looks like you've got her figured,' Bobby commented.

'I wouldn't go that far,' Storm said, 'but I've got her interest — that's for sure.'

'You called her Clara, is that her real name?'

'Yes. It seems to kind of unnerve her

when I use it, I don't know why. You ought to try it on your girl — it at least gets them to thinking.'

'I suppose it would,' Bobby said. 'At least it might set me apart a little from the herd of range-riding men she serves every day. It couldn't hurt, I suppose.'

'Might even help. I can see you're fond of the woman, Bobby, and would like to get fonder. Why don't you try calling her Sheila when she comes back to the table?'

Clara Fine came back shortly with Storm's meal, since it was the special for that night and took no undue preparation time. She did not speak and neither did Storm, but she smiled, just faintly — a little twitch of the corner of her mouth which even Bobby Ryder saw.

'I'm feeling better,' Bobby said, leaning back with a toothpick between his lips, his plate clean. 'What now? I can't imagine a hangman has any work to do on this night.'

'No, a hangman wouldn't,' Storm

agreed. 'But a deputy sheriff might be looking ahead to a crimson sunset followed by flame and thunder.'

'Tell me about it,' Bobby Ryder said, leaning forward across the table, his eyes intent; so Storm did.

Storm glanced at the sundown sky as the two stepped out the front door of Zebulon's. Then, glancing down the street he said, 'There's still somebody at the bank.'

'That will be Colin Pierce. He keeps strict hours.'

Storm nodded. 'I still haven't talked to him. I should do that now while he's available. Why don't you make your way on over to the jail? Taffy is behind it or alongside it somewhere, watching from the alley. Call out before you walk into where it's dark. He's not expecting any pleasant company. Take your rifle — I'll be along as soon as I've finished with Pierce. That should give us enough men to stand them off.'

'We're expecting trouble tonight then?'

'We are. They're determined to break Nate Lydell out and hang him tonight. Determined enough that there's someone ready to try dynamite.'

'Dynamite! That would . . . '

'Yes, it would, wouldn't it?' Storm said with a rueful smile. 'We'll not let them get close enough to the jail to try using it. Still want this job, Bobby?'

'Yes, I do. Anybody who's crazy enough to try that stunt needs to be stopped.'

'Get going then. I'll be seeing you soon. Stay alert.'

'Wouldn't anybody, knowing that there were men out there who'd like to blow you apart?'

'You'd think so, but there have been hundreds of cases of sentries falling asleep, haven't there? Oh Bobby, if Taffy wants to go get some food and coffee, that's fine. I don't expect the Belvedere crew to come out of the saloon until later when they're good and drunk and the streets have been cleared of civilians.'

'Around midnight — you're probably right there, Storm.' Bobby's expression grew more concerned. 'You know it was bad enough that Nate was in jail in the first place, now Jocko Lydell himself is being held. If anyone does try anything more against the marshal's office, the Corkscrew boys are bound to come riding in to take them both into their own kind of custody.'

'We can't help that. I wish we could make Corkscrew see that their sort of help would be no help at all. Nate and Jocko would just be tracked down and rearrested.'

Bobby Ryder's comment was only a low, muttered curse and Storm started for the bank, wanting to catch Colin Pierce, the bank teller, before he left. There might be something to be found out from him. What, Storm couldn't guess. He only knew that as of now his investigation was only swinging in the wind; things were progressing no more quickly than they would have had he never arrived in King's Creek.

Tying his black horse up to the hitch rail in front of the bank, Storm stepped on to the plank walk and knocked at the door. There was a golden haze of light still in the sundown sky. But soon it would be pitch dark, and then Randy Travis and his crew could begin planning their own method of colouring the sky — with the red flaring of explosives. What Storm had told Bobby was what he believed — the raiders would not make their move this early in the evening with the streets still crowded with shoppers from the farms, cattlemen, teamsters and mine workers.

That was what he believed, but you never knew, did you?

No one had answered his knock so he rattled the knob on the door. Still no one came to answer. The lantern within, turned low, still burned and Storm was sure someone was there. In this country with all-wood construction, fire was a grave concern to everyone. Untended lanterns weren't left burning.

Storm bent low, peered, thought he saw a moving silhouette behind the bank counter, rapped again and received a timorous answer.

'Who is it?'

'The law — I need to talk to you, Pierce!'

'What about?'

'Open up and I'll tell you.'

Obviously Pierce did not want to answer the door. Probably he wanted no more trouble from anyone for a while. That was just too bad. Storm rapped again, loudly, and he was rewarded with the sound of approaching footsteps.

The door opened a scant few inches and the narrow, worried face of Colin Pierce appeared in the dim light. His hair was neatly brushed back, his eyes were wide behind rimless spectacles. His small mouth was decorated with a closely clipped moustache. His suit was as neat as those worn by bankers everywhere. There was a burgundy coloured tie wrapped around his throat.

'I don't . . . who are you?' Pierce

asked in a voice that had developed a squeak. The man was obviously still shaken by recent events. Storm knew he would have to announce himself sooner or later to the town, and this seemed the right time so he removed his badge from the inner pocket of his coat and showed it to the uncertain Pierce.

'County Sheriff's office, Hiller.'

That didn't surprise Pierce as much as he had expected, but then he considered that Colin Pierce had never had any contact with him as the hangman either. What the badge did gain for Storm was a hesitant smile, a look of relief, and entry to the bank.

There were two captain's chairs in the lobby facing each other across a small round table, and Storm took one of these without having been invited. Colin Pierce assumed the other.

'I know why you're here,' Pierce said, looking up doubtfully from behind his spectacles.

'If you have been keeping up with the recent doings in King's Creek, you know that Marshal Bean hasn't had the time to do a lot of investigating concerning the bank robbery. I have the time. Why don't you tell me about it?'

Pierce leaned back in his chair, sighed, inspected an imaginary speck on his glasses, put them back on and began. 'I can't really tell you much, Hiller. Nothing I haven't told the marshal, that is. I came to work Monday morning at the usual time and found the safe standing open.'

'Patrick Teasdale hadn't come in yet?'

'No. I didn't expect him, either. He'd been at a business meeting down in Sexton all weekend, and he would have just gotten back that morning. He wouldn't have rushed over — Mr Teasdale had ultimate faith in my abilities . . . and look where that got us!' Pierce moaned. For a minute Storm thought the young teller was going to start crying, but he knuckled his eyes and sat there staring miserably at Storm.

'There wasn't a thing I could have

done to prevent the robbery,' Pierce said.

'No, I don't see what if you weren't even at the bank at the time.'

'That's the same thing Mr Teasdale told me later. 'There's nothing you could have done, Colin. No need to blame yourself.''

'You saw immediately that there was money missing from the safe?'

'Yes, immediately. There was no other reason for the safe door to be standing open, was there? But I went to it and examined the cash drawers. It was gone, all of it excepting the silver.'

'There was no evidence that the safe had been tampered with.'

'None. No sign that tools had been used on it, nothing like that, and it obviously hadn't been blasted open.'

'Not many try that anymore. It would bring the whole town running. It can ruin a lot of whatever is in the safe — if they even manage to open it, which is a long shot unless you're exceptionally skilled with explosives. Not many are.'

Storm paused, then said, 'Patrick Teasdale was said to be the only one who knew the combination to that safe.'

'That's true,' Pierce answered, his expression now a little uncertain.

'What were you to do if Teasdale became incapacitated? Got sick, fell off his horse, bitten by a snake, run out to his house — ask him for it?'

'No, things were a little more complicated than that — even if they would have been just as fast.

'The company that made the safe has a record of the combination, obviously. If they were notified by telegraph, the combination could be sent to an authorized possessor of a certain code — that I do have access to.'

'And if you did ever have to do that, the whole town would know about it.'

'I'm afraid so . . . ' Pierce was glum again. 'But Hiller, if you're thinking . . . '

'I'm not thinking you had anything to do with this, if that's what you're going to say. I just wanted to establish that no

114

one else could have come by that combination.'

'No one could have.'

Hiller was satisfied. If Janet Teasdale hadn't been involved. He had run into that mental brick wall again.

'About Teasdale, are we certain he was out of town?'

'Of course!' the question seemed to confound Pierce and somehow offend him. 'I can give you a list of the men he was meeting with in Sexton. I can assure you they are well-respected and all can vouch for Mr Teasdale's presence at the conference. Just ask them!'

'There isn't the time, now that they've all scattered to the winds. Don't bother about that list — I already have it mentally. Most of them were local businessmen, weren't they?'

Pierce frowned as if Storm were implying something. He was, of course, in a way. He was simply investigating.

'Yes,' Pierce eventually answered. 'Mr Dawson who owns the freight line attended and Buck Dewar, the copper mine owner. They are both based in King's Creek.'

'Are both of their businesses flourishing?' Storm asked and Pierce's already tight face drew tighter with exasperation.

'Both are among our largest depositors. Why would you ask?'

'You never know. It's my job to ask awkward questions,' Storm Hiller said. It was an explanation, not an apology. These two, then, apparently had no need to take risks for the sake of profit.

'And the Sexton City Bank is solvent?'

'Of course!' Pierce looked offended once more. 'Why are you asking questions like these?'

'Well, the meeting was held in Sexton and . . . '

'And your imagination started running away with you,' Pierce said stiffly. 'All of that is misleading and asinine — as you have pointed out, the safe could only be opened by Mr Teasdale.'

'Who could not have opened it because he was in Sexton.'

'Yes.' Pierce's face was briefly smug. Then he realized he had confounded himself. He shrugged as if to indicate he was bowing out of the conversation, and stood. He added as they walked toward the door, 'I can assure you that the safe was locked before Mr Teasdale left for Sexton. We checked it together when Mr Dewar arrived to meet him.'

'The mine boss went to Sexton with him?'

'Of course, they were friendly, and were both riding to the same conference. Mr Dewar arrived promptly at noon with his man, Cooper, and the three left together at that time.'

Storm had a sensation like ice creeping up his spine. He halted and demanded of Pierce, 'Did you say Handy Cooper rode off with the two men?'

'I think that was his name. Cooper, yes. Apparently he works for Mr Dewar as a guard at the mine. He said he'd feel safer with a little extra protection on the long trail, and I must say Mr Cooper certainly had the look of a competent man.'

Yes, you could say Handy Cooper was competent. You could ask any of the six men he had killed in gunfights if he was not handy with a Colt.

Storm had run out of questions, and Pierce had run out of answers. He started to say goodbye and offer Pierce his thanks, but before he could get to the pleasantries, there was a furious pounding on the bank's door and they heard Bobby Ryder's voice raised there.

'Storm! Better get out here — the Belvedere Saloon crowd is making its move.'

7

As soon as he had reached the plank walk Storm could hear the angry, mutinous sounds of many voices. It was not a pretty sound. Now and then an encouraging cheer rose. The men walked on steadily, approaching the jail. Storm could easily see that all of them were armed.

'Do you know where Taffy is?'

'On the far side, in the alley.'

Oretheon Bean would be at his window, peering out from a slotted window cut in the heavy shutters.

'Let's check the back first to make sure there aren't more of them sneaking up that way.'

Bobby Ryder only nodded. He was probably already mulling over the question of how he could shoot down men he knew, some perhaps friends of his. Storm was untroubled by such worries, he still hated the idea of being forced to gun down citizens of King's Creek. He didn't want things this way, but that's the way it was.

When they had taken up guns against the law, they had made outlaws of themselves.

Storm and Bobby circled carefully but swiftly toward the rear of the jail, passing silently through the oak shadows. There was no force there; no one had considered dispatching men that way. If they had, all were reluctant to miss the big show — an explosion of dynamite sending the jail collapsing to the ground in a wash of falling bricks and dropping timbers, with the sheriff and the two men inside condemned to death.

'Where's Taffy?'

'Far side of the jail, in the other alley. Right near to Nate Lydell's cell window,' Bobby replied in a pant as they continued to jog on.

The mob in the street had grown closer, louder, the almost animal sounds they made surging over them, Storm made his way to the front of the alley where he could peer out and watch the Belvedere Saloon men approaching to execute their plan which to them seemed utterly necessary. Now Storm could make out two or three faces, but he knew none of them.

'Who's got the dynamite?' Bobby, now beside him hissed, gripping his Winchester tightly with both hands.

'I can't tell. Bobby, could they have been bluffing about that?'

'These boys don't go in much for bluffs,' Bobby answered in a throaty voice. He was obviously feeling the stress.

'If we could spot the man with the dynamite . . . ' Storm said. There was no need to continue with his sentence. Bobby Ryder knew what he was thinking. He also knew that it would require taking out the man from hiding, shooting him down before the hostilities had begun. There was something slightly cowardly about it, looked at that way. On the other hand, it was an utterly stupid tactic to let them draw nearer with explosives.

'Maybe Bean will see him,' Bobby said hopefully, as if he would not mind it so much if the marshal was the one who had to shoot the bomber.

A smaller group of men within the mass of raiders had gathered around a central figure. A match was lighted, flaring up to briefly illuminate the tense faces of the men. Storm knew it was then or never. He shouldered his rifle and shot the man with the dynamite before that match could be touched to the fuse.

Men were suddenly firing wildly, scattering in all directions. Storm had hoped the men would give it up and disperse, but that was not what they were doing. Even as Taffy opened up with his rifle from the far alley and Oretheon Bean began shooting through the flung open shutter on his window, the men were firing back at the jail house. Up and down the street, stabbing flame from the muzzles of their weapons could be easily seen in the night, and two close bullets sang off the jail wall not far from Storm's head. A couple more slugs hit the front door of the jail with dull thudding sounds. No, they had not given up their assault, but withdrawing to re-form.

Storm realized what had happened only as a remaining man tried to stamp on the fuse to the bundle of dynamite. The man with the match had succeeded in touching fire to it after all. Seeing that the fuse was short, that he was probably too late, the Belvedere man gave it up and sprinted madly for cover.

Storm saw the deadly sparking of the fuse and lowered his head, placing a hand on Bobby's shoulder to hold him back. Taffy had now appeared at the head of the other alley and was using his Winchester to keep the attackers scurrying. Storm tried to yell out a warning, but he was too late.

The dynamite went off with a

brilliant flare of light which must have flooded the sky for miles around and a deep, rumbling explosion sounded. Storm pawed at his eyes which stung, itched, teared and burned. He could see nothing but a stunningly bright yellow orb for long seconds; his ears rang with the echo of the blast and his head throbbed wildly. For a minute he could not focus any of his senses.

The dry, heated wash of the explosion swept over them, the force of the dynamite explosion thrusting at Storm's body, forcing him back a step or two. His shirt flapped wildly in the wake of the blast. Bobby Ryder was down on his knees, his hands covering his ears. Useless, since there would not be a second blast, but it is an ancient reaction, like ducking from a bullet that has already been fired. Men tend to react defensively as their hairy ancestors did in times of trouble, though the attackers had progressed from hurling rocks to bullets and dynamite.

At the same time the sky had begun

raining debris on them. Pieces of wood, some afire, chips of building blocks, dirt, glass, gravel and fragments of metal. As these continued to fall — the lighter pieces now — Storm looked out from their sheltering place and saw that the explosion had taken out the front window of the saddlery, and nearer to the blast, the front of the hardware store had been nearly destroyed. Its awning, the uprights, no longer standing, bowed its capitulation.

In the centre of this destruction, a crater had been created in the middle of the street. Smoke wafted up from it. Along the street men issued out into the night, surveying the damage, wailing with distress as they viewed the destruction. A voice nearby was lifted in cries of pain and anger. Storm was sure it came from the other alley on the far side of the jail, the side closer to the blast.

'Come on,' Storm said, slapping Bobby Ryder's shoulder, 'I think they got Taffy.'

That was indeed what had happened; rushing around the front of the jail, they entered the destruction on that side. Scattered adobe blocks lay in jumbles before the gaping hole blasted into the wall of the jail house. There were still wisps of smoke from the explosion, forming wreaths along the alley.

Taffy was trapped beneath a pile of rubble which had rained down on him. He was trying futilely to free his right leg from the stack of littered bricks which held it pinned. The leg was bent at an unnatural angle, his yellow hair was singed off, his face blackened where the red of blood did not show.

'Help's here,' Storm said with a smile as if Taffy's predicament was only a nuisance and not a threat to his life and limb. Taffy nodded his thanks and let his head fall back against the alley floor. Storm began moving the heaviest of the block segments from Taffy's leg, trying not to cause another movement to jolt the limb which seemed to be critically injured. Noticing that he was working alone, Storm glanced up and saw Bobby Ryder standing stock still, staring at a cavern mouth carved into the jail house wall. It gaped there as a sort of jagged archway decorated with a twisted iron bar. Nathan Lydell stood staring silently back at him. Did he believe in that dazed, smoke-filled moment that his friend Bobby Ryder had come to spring him from his cell? It didn't matter what Nate thought. Behind him, the corridor of the jail could be clearly seen, and standing there with his pistol unlimbered stood Marshal Oretheon Bean. The marshal called out toward the darkness, 'Deputy Hiller?'

'It's me, Oretheon. Taffy's got himself pinned. We've a little work to do here.'

'Pinned?'

'About half a ton of adobe bricks fell on his leg. We've almost got him out,' Storm called, which was far from the truth but it did no harm to cheer the marshal and especially Taffy a little.

'If they've crippled him . . . ' they

heard Bean mutter, then louder, 'You get back in the far corner.'

This order was obviously meant for young Nate Lydell, who nodded and moved away from the hole in the side of the jail. Nate's eyes were glassy, his movements uncertain. Storm thought the kid had been addled some by the force of the near blast.

At least, he could tell himself, the mob hadn't gotten any closer to dragging Nate out and stringing him up. With the man already condemned, with his 'hangman' in town, Storm was left to wonder what all the haste was about in making sure the young man died quickly. Nate had remained silent all through his trial, they said; was it that someone feared that the nearness of death might prompt Nate to speak now and save his neck?

What could he possibly have to say that had remained secret up to now and someone saw as a threat?

King's Creek had its problems and its secrets, that was for sure, but they were tangled up in a way that thwarted Storm Hiller's understanding of them. And so he could find no solution to them.

Storm rocked back on his heels as he crouched over Taffy in the dark alley, finally beckoning to Ryder who had wisely taken up a sentry position at the head of the alley. Men as wild as the Belvedere mob were unlikely to just go home and to bed, forgetting about things.

'I think we can move him now,' Storm told Bobby. Turning to the jail house he called, 'Bean, are you still there?'

'Still here.'

'Good. What about if we bring Taffy in this way instead of risking passing the front of the jail? There could be snipers out there.'

'Sounds like a better way,' Oretheon Bean agreed. 'Wait until I unlock the cell door, then just bring Taffy through. You can put him down on my bunk in the back room.'

And so they did, Taffy moaning only a little. He seemed unable to complain more. His strength was trickling away with his blood. After placing him carefully on the marshal's bunk, Storm cut away the leg of the deputy's trousers. The flesh beneath it was bloody, torn, the bone impossibly shattered, one sharp fragment poking through the skin.

'He won't make it without a doctor,' Storm said in what was an understatement — it was doubtful that any doctor could save that leg, or Taffy's life. Oretheon Bean had fallen into a spasm of cursing and vowing retribution. It did no good of course to stand and swear so Storm grabbed the marshal's arm and said in an urgent tone, 'He needs that doctor now!'

Oretheon's eyes cleared of rage and settled to a practical gaze. 'I know it, Storm; why don't you go find the man? I obviously can't leave the jail now.'

'What are you going to do with Nathan?'

'I'll give him his wish and put him in with his father. Now,' Oretheon said, 'go get that doctor.'

'Send Bobby,' Storm said, resisting Marshal Bean's command.

'Why?'

'Two reasons I can think of: Bobby knows where the man lives, I don't.'

'What's the second reason?' Oretheon wanted to know.

'Those Belvedere men have gotten away with too much for too long, they believe that they've weakened the law so much that they now have free rein to do as they please. I'm going to take the message to them that the law in King's Creek is still functioning. They've committed attempted murder of a peace officer — we can't be having that.' Storm nodded at Taffy, who was resting uncomfortably on the bunk, the life probably leaking from him.

'We don't even know for sure who it was,' the marshal objected.

'We know who was behind it — Randy Travis, or am I wrong?'

'No, you're right about that, Storm, but what are we going to do with him even if you could find him and arrest him? We've got no room for more prisoners.'

'I'll keep that in mind,' Storm Hiller said in a cold voice, and for the first time Oretheon Bean could remember, there was no smile following the hard statement. For it was Storm's intention to visit retribution on Randy Travis, and to remind the man if necessary, that there were other ways to die than at the end of a rope. It seemed to Bobby Ryder that Storm had now shed any pretence of being the man with the rope and had become again what he actually was — a lawman with a ready six-gun.

As if to emphasize that valuation, Storm removed his badge from his pocket and pinned it on to the front of his white shirt.

'Better go get that doctor,' Storm said to Bobby who had not left yet.

'One minute, Storm,' Oretheon Bean said worriedly. 'If you're leaving and Ryder's going, that leaves me in a bit of a mess, considering I now have an open back door.'

'It won't take Bobby long to get back.'

'I thought we agreed that he wouldn't remain in the jail. Ryder's still a Corkscrew man, you know?'

'I am,' Bobby said a little hotly, 'and I hope the boys make their move to defend Nathan and the boss, and bring plenty of powder and lead to do it, but I'm not with them whatever they have decided to do.' He looked levelly at Storm and then at Marshal Bean. 'I am a man with a badge now. I didn't take no oath but I gave Storm my word and I mean to stand by what I said.'

'Go get the doctor,' Storm ordered. 'We're debating pointlessly while a man is lying here, hurt badly.'

Bobby started to answer, changed his mind and slipped out of the jail using the side opening as a door once again.

'What am I supposed to do with Bobby Ryder now?' Bean asked querulously.

'Nothing at all,' Storm answered, 'or anything you please. The man's given his word; if you don't choose to take him at it, you can push him out again, but that would leave you completely alone against the night and the Belvedere mob. It seems to me that you'd be better off taking any help you can get while it's still being offered.'

Oretheon Bean thought it over as he escorted young Nate to the back of the corridor where Jocko Lydell, who had been shouting questions since this had all begun, waited for his son.

And Storm Hiller, without even the hint of a smile, slipped out through the jagged, gaping wall to take his own chances at facing the night and the Belvedere gang.

8

The night was like some sleeping ghost in the streets of King's Creek. After the shattering sound of the explosion earlier, the streets had returned to silence. But the ghost was not sleeping — this ghost had a body with veins of violence running through it hotly; it had only paused for a moment to gather its mortal strength again.

There were other creatures in the night, men who sneaked about shadow to shadow like jackals waiting to attack, maim and kill. As every animal has its prey, so everyone has its hunter. The jackals did not know it yet, but there was a stealthy night-hunter among them. They knew him as a hangman, but he was even more deadly with a pistol in his hand.

It was a good weapon for his kind of hunting: a Colt revolver.

Storm moved into an alley where there was less chance of his being seen, and continued making his way toward the Belvedere Saloon, the watering hole where the jackals congregated. It seemed that he had spent all of his time in King's Creek in one alleyway or another. He walked steadily, but not hurriedly, on. He was passing a closed alleyside door when a hand reached out and clutched his arm.

'Where are you going?' a familiar voice asked. Storm, who had had his gun halfway drawn, now relaxed his grip as he recognized the unexpected face of Clara Fine looking up at him from the darkness.

'Hunting,' was his terse reply.

'I have to . . . you'd better step in here,' she said, her dark eyes darting up and down the alley. A tug on his arm emphasized her words and he side-stepped into a small, narrow room which was illuminated only dimly by a light beyond the door. It seemed to be the storage room of Zebulon's restaurant, crowded with brooms, mops and pails.

'What is it?' Storm demanded, his eyes narrow and cautious. He did not like being trapped in a confined space even with a girl as pretty as Clara as it left little room for manoeuvering. Clara was obviously tense. Her arms were crossed and though she tilted against the side wall of the storage room, she looked uncomfortable. Her mouth was uneasy, tight.

'What are you doing out there, Storm?' she asked, using his name for the first time that he could recall. 'It has something to do with that explosion, doesn't it?' Her finger reached out and just touched the shining shield on his shirt.

'It has everything to do with it,' Storm answered. 'What may have started out as a mere disagreement between various factions in this town has degenerated into a riot where men think nothing of hurling dynamite at each other.'

'I know. Tell me, Storm, where is Bobby Ryder?'

'He's at the marshal's office with Bean.'

'But he's a . . .'

'He's a Corkscrew man, I know, and a friend of Nate Lydell. Oretheon knows it, too, but though he doesn't like it much, Ryder is the nearest thing to a deputy he's been able to find in this hobbled town.'

'So long as Bobby's all right,' Clara said. 'When the explosion went off, everyone became frightened about who might have been injured.'

'He's all right for now. Who knows what they have planned next? Why should you worry so much about Bobby?'

'Oh, it wasn't me! But Sheila Porter has been beside herself with worry.'

'Over Bobby?'

'She's crazy about him, Storm.' Clara touched the sleeve of his shirt again, eyes looking up almost eagerly.

'Bobby doesn't know that. She could at least give him a smile. A touch of encouragement would go a long way.'

'I know. She knows. It's just that often in the past we have spent so much time discouraging certain sorts of men.' Her eyes dropped and her hand fell from his sleeve.

'Certain sorts?'

'Oh, you know. Rowdies, outlaws, common cowboys.'

'You lump them all together,' Storm said, 'what's the matter with pushing cows for a living?'

'Nothing — for them — but it doesn't really promise a woman much to look forward to, does it?'

'I suppose not.'

'I hear them all the time talking about how they're going to leave and start their own little ranch someday. Do you know how many ever can do that?'

'Only a few.'

'Yes, and that's the end of their ambition,' Clara said as if with frustration. 'Can you imagine what life is like for a woman dragged along to start a ranch from bare ground with no money for stock, for shelter, even for food?

With no warmth in the winter, without a single neighbour to talk to?'

'A woman would really have to be in love,' Storm said.

'So much so that it bordered on insanity, made her blind to the struggles ahead after the honeymoon ended.'

'So you and Sheila have taken a vow never to walk into any such situation?'

'Exactly! Storm, do you truthfully think we're wrong about that?'

'Depends on how you look at things, I guess.' He paused. 'But no, I can't say that you're wrong. Life has enough risks just living day to day, why explore new ones?'

'Exactly,' Clara said with relief. It was as if she had finally taught a slow student to grasp her point. 'There are certain sorts of men that I would never consider marrying, even though I might like them well enough — men with no ambition whatsoever. Also men with unsavoury jobs . . . like a hangman. I could never consider marrying a hangman or a mortician.'

'Well then, it's a good thing you don't have any of those pursuing you, isn't it?' Storm said a little sharply, 'Since you'd fall back on your prejudice and dismiss him at first meeting.'

'But you're neither, are you?' Clara said, nodding at the badge.

'No,' he said, still with some heat. What was he angry about? Her earlier attitude toward him — it had to be. Storm gathered himself again and asked Clara, 'All right, then, why did you stop me and bring me in here? It can't have been just to discuss your personal affairs.'

'No. It's a quite vital matter, Storm. We may still be able to smooth things over in this town before you set off to shoot down all of Nate's enemies, all of Oretheon Bean's — it couldn't be done anyway, could it? There are packs of them.'

'You have a better way to bring peace?'

'I think so . . . maybe.' She now held the fabric of his shirt with both hands.

Clara hesitated, shook her head, and told him, 'Storm, I know where Janet Teasdale is.'

He simply stood there for a long minute, looking down into her shadowed face. The clutch of her fingers on his shirt fell away and her hands lowered. Her expression was now of one shamed.

Quite softly, with the voice of a man rigidly controlling his tone, he said, 'I heard you right, didn't I? You know where Janet Teasdale is?'

'Yes,' she answered in a whisper. Her eyes remained downcast; Storm lifted her chin with his thumb.

'And the girl is alive?'

'Oh yes, she's quite alive.' Her liquid eyes were fixed on his. Shame still lingered there. And a little bit of fear.

'Why did it take you till now to speak up? Were you waiting to see how many people might be killed in this bloody commotion?'

'No, Storm,' she said, her eyes still turned down toward the floorboards of the storage room. 'How could I speak up? It wasn't my place.'

'Whose place was it then?'

'Janet's, of course, or possibly Nate's, but certainly not mine.'

'You'd rather watch an innocent man hang?'

'I couldn't do that. I suppose if it came down to that I would have to tell folks if Nate hadn't himself yet. I just don't know if they'd believe me if I rushed up on to the scaffold.'

'It would probably be too late,' Storm agreed. 'I've got to give Nate some credit, if he gave his word not to reveal Janet's hiding place, no matter what, he sure kept his promise.'

'Of course he would for Janet.'

'What happened, Clara? Janet wasn't kidnapped, was she?' Storm had been holding out that possibility for a while. She would have given the bank robbers considerable leverage over Patrick Teasdale. They could have held her hostage, promising her release in return for the bank vault's combination.

'No, of course not,' Clara answered,

Why 'of course not'? No matter, that concern had been done away with. There was only one other possibility, Storm thought.

'Then she ran away and is in hiding, even with Nathan Lydell's life hanging in the balance?'

'Yes, that's it. She never really thought they would sentence him to be hanged since they had no dead body to use to convict him.'

'Well, she was wrong, wasn't she?' Storm said coldly. 'Leave it at that for the moment. Clara, you have to know why Janet is in hiding. I need to know, and I need to know now. This town hasn't even begun to tear itself apart. That dynamite was just the opening declaration of war. It'll be sure to bring the Corkscrew crew to town, seeing that they know now that the marshal can't protect Nate and Jocko from Randy Travis and that lynch mob.

'Why is she hiding, Clara? Just tell me that much and maybe I can get to the bottom of this mess and save Nathan Lydell's neck along the way.'

'That is what I can't tell you, Storm. I gave my word. Only Janet can tell you.'

'This is getting us nowhere, Clara. The only way to begin untangling things is for you to take me to wherever Janet is and I'll ask her to save Nate and help me fight back the savages in this town. There's no other choice. Will you take me to see her?'

She was a long time considering, but in the end Clara Fine nodded her head, and as they heard rifle shots sounding from uptown, she told Storm, 'Let's get going. I'll take you to Janet Teasdale. You're right; I think this is the only way, too.'

And if Janet didn't wish to return to King's Creek, that was just too bad, Storm was thinking as they stepped out into the cool, gunfire-filled night. If she did not wish to return, she was coming anyway, Storm vowed. He was saving King's Creek and Nate Lydell from themselves, whether they wished it or not. If he had to hog-tie Janet Teasdale and bring her in over his horse's back, she was coming. Before the whole town was wrapped up in smoke and flames pierced only by flying lead.

Storm was able to recover his black horse from the stable without any opposition. Meeting with Clara Fine who waited on her dun pony, they headed southward, away from gunfire. Storm glanced back only once. The whole damned town seemed to be willing to destroy itself, to burn it to the ground if need be to reach one uncertain goal. He had seen worse riots — Studdardville, for example — but there had been a lot more at stake in that fight. These men were violence unleashed and mindless, a mad dog biting itself on the butt, so eager was it to attack something, someone. That's what riots were about. That and not really knowing why they were fighting, which was another hallmark of mindless mobs.

The trail south was visible in the pale glow of the rising moon. Black, featureless oaks, stark against the dark sky, lined their way. They barely spoke. Storm heard the riders coming before he saw them, and he touched Clara's arm and guided her back among the night-oaks, reaching the heavy shadows there as the boiling group of horsemen drove their horses at speed toward King's Creek. They watched silently until the riders had passed by.

'Where were they going in such a rush?' Clara asked, She had recognized a few of the men from her work at Zebulon's.

'Were they Corkscrew men?' Storm asked, although he already knew the answer.

'Yes,' Clara said a little breathlessly, her eyes bright in the night. 'Where could they be going at such a pace?'

'They're going to add fuel to the fire,' Storm growled. They could still hear distant gunshots from the town. Soon there would be more, by the hundreds, and justice having been done or not, King's Creek would be brought to its knees. 'Let's keep going,' he added, 'we can do nothing for those left in town.'

Not without Janet Teasdale there to tell her story. And what was her story, exactly? Storm thought he had already heard and discarded the most likely and prevalent of them. He heeled his horse, hurrying its pace a little, forcing Clara to keep up with him.

Now deep into Corkscrew territory, he pulled his horse back and said, 'Enough! Where are we going?'

'To Aunt Gretel's, of course,' Clara said, as if any child would have known. But Storm, who knew nothing of the area, little of local inhabitants at least, finally had the first hint at solving the mystery.

'She's Teasdale's sister?'

'Of course not,' Clara said in that same weary school teacher way she had. He would have to do something about that . . . he shook his head. What was he thinking? All he needed to be worrying

148

about right now was Janet Teasdale. Clara was still talking. ' . . . so we agreed that Janet should go to Sheila's aunt's house. It was near enough and no one would think to look for her there.'

'Aunt Gretel is Sheila Porter's aunt?'

'That's what I just said, isn't it?'

'What does she call herself — Leticia Saltcod?'

'That's not funny!'

'I thought all of the women in this secret club of yours had false names. Never mind,' Storm said sharply. 'Let's get there, now, while there's still time.'

★ ★ ★

The sweat was raining off Oretheon Bean's forehead. He stood at the window slit now, firing the last two rounds in his Winchester's magazine at darting shadows up the street. It was the second rifle he had emptied. He snatched a third from the gun rack and flickered a glance toward the now-demolished cell where Bobby Ryder was still shooting, holding off an attack from that side.

He heard a man's scream from the back alley, so Bobby's shooting was having some effect on keeping them back. Oretheon fired at an approaching shadow, missed and jacked a new cartridge into the receiver of the Winchester. There was a spate of firing at the rear of the jail, shots from the outside, apparently hitting nothing but adobe bricks and iron.

'God's sake, Bean!' Jocko Lydell hollered. 'They're shooting at the window to our cell. Let us out or give me a gun to protect myself. What did I do to deserve this?'

'Nothing,' the marshal yelled back, 'except to try to do the same thing to another man, a deputy sheriff!'

'I know I did, and I'm sorry about that, Bean. I didn't know who he was. I assumed . . . I was out of my mind. I needed to keep Nate alive. You'd fight for your own pup, wouldn't you?'

'I don't think I'd stoop to waylaying strangers in alleys,' Bean said, fixing his sights on another outside target. He squeezed off a shot, missed again, and cussed as his target dove from sight.

'You told me you'd let me out when Deputy Hiller was gone,' Jocko continued, 'well, he's gone now, isn't he? How about it, Bean?'

'He'll be back,' the marshal said. He was trying hard to ignore Jocko Lydell's pleading, but outside the window, Bean could see new knots of shadowy men forming in the darkness, moving forward in the night. Always forward. These men would not give up. He and Bobby Ryder could not hold them back forever . . .

The sound of approaching horses at the head of the street shifted Bean's attention that way. He breathed out a violent oath and said aloud, 'That clears the table.'

'What's that?' Jocko Lydell called. 'I don't understand you.'

Everything had just changed. It was the Corkscrew riders arriving; Bean could tell as he recognized a man or two. The scene outside changed from a raid on the jail to an out and out military-style conflict. The battle lines had been drawn, and now the Corkscrew riders and the Belvedere men settled in for what was bound to be a grim and deadly war.

Bean was left in a precarious position. The Corkscrew men had momentarily driven back the soldiers of Randy Travis, but they would regroup. Meanwhile, the marshal was in the position of having to protect his prisoners from the one gang while preventing the other from releasing them, and his only help in this battle was Bobby Ryder, who also rode for the Corkscrew brand.

Damn it! He could use the assistance of Storm Hiller at this moment, but Bean had no idea where the deputy had gotten to, if he was even still alive. With one eye on the damaged cell where Bobby Ryder had been trying to hold the fort against the Belvedere mob, the marshal settled behind his iron sights and triggered off a few more, probably futile rounds after the routed Belvedere men.

He could do nothing more. Outside, the night was in chaos and he was pinned in the jail house like one more prisoner to be saved — or executed — at the whim of the winner of the gun battle which threatened to tear the heart out of King's Creek that night.

Where could Storm Hiller be?

9

The sound of the gunfight had been swallowed by distance, although Storm had no doubt that the battle for King's Creek was continuing. The solution to it all may rest in the small cabin they viewed now from the surrounding wooded hills. Storm had to convince himself that it did, that the supposedly dead Janet Teasdale was down there with her secret — whatever it was — that would potentially save many lives, including the life of her supposed lover, Nate Lydell.

'It's awful quiet down there,' he commented to Clara Fine.

'People back here don't stay up late — there's no point in it'

'No, and being roused from their beds on a night like this is bound to bring confusion and not a little bit of anger. However, that is what we came for and we'd better go down and see to it.'

Storm let Clara lead the way down the mountain slope where the moonlight through the pines struck in irregular patches against the cold earth. A prowling coyote was startled from their path as they descended toward the valley floor through the timber, following a winding path. As they reached the narrow hidden meadow and turned their horses toward the cabin, a diving, broad-winged owl swooped past their heads. Storm was glad he did not believe in omens.

The cabin, of unbarked logs, was not as empty or abandoned as it had appeared from the ridge, for now Storm could see lamplight bleeding out through a high window in the back wall. He pointed it out to Clara.

'Someone's awake.'

She nodded, but did not seem pleased. Her expression had grown more glum as their ride progressed. Storm guessed that she was feeling guilty about breaking her oath of silence.

'You're doing the right thing, Clara,' Storm told her with a smile which seemed to revive her spirits a little.

'I know it — but even so . . . I did give my word.'

'When Janet hears the explanation, she'll tell you it was the right thing to do as well.'

Clara took in a deep breath and let it out slowly. 'I hope so.' As they crossed the yard toward the cabin, Clara said, 'You'd better let me approach the house alone. They won't know who you are and it won't do to frighten them.'

Storm nodded agreement and reined in his black horse. 'You're right. Go ahead.'

As Storm watched, shivering a little as the cold wind filtered through the trees, Clara rode to the front of the cabin, swung down from her dun pony and walked to the front door of the cabin. She glanced back at him once and then resolutely knocked on the door.

It was swung open a crack and

lantern light bled out, painting a narrow yellow ribbon against the dark earth. Storm heard a small sound of surprise and then the door was flung wide. A stout, middle-aged woman in a blue housecoat stood there, and she welcomed Clara with a hug.

Storm could hear mingled, excited words pass between them. Then Clara said something else and pointed toward where Storm was waiting. A few more gabbled words were exchanged and Clara turned to motion Storm forward.

Still uncertain of the situation, Storm walked his horse forward, his eyes flickering one way and the other, searching for any possible threat lurking in the darkness. Men called him overly-cautious, but his manner had kept him alive for this long. He did not mean to be shot down, ambushed in the night as he approached this small woodland cabin.

He knew a few men who were completely comfortable taking care of their business that way.

Clara and Aunt Gretel — that was who the older woman had to be — had moved inside the house, but both were still visible through the doorway which stood open for Storm. He tied up the horses and went in, dusting himself off with his hat.

Storm was introduced to Aunt Gretel, a short, square woman with grey hair escaping her night cap. Her mouth was tight, puckered; her blue eyes bright and inquisitive. Her expression seemed to have loosened when she saw the badge on Storm's shirt front; nevertheless, she appeared a little apprehensive.

The introduction had hardly been completed when Storm heard a muffled sound, and looking that way, saw an interior door opening. A young, red-haired woman in a night dress and short jacket appeared, moving with painful slowness.

'Clara!' she called out, rushing across the space between them to hug Clara Fine, her eyes on Storm Hiller. The girl did not look like one who had been

158

resting comfortably. There was a harried, haunted look in her eyes.

'Janet Teasdale?' Storm asked.

'Yes,' a small voice answered.

'The game is over. We have to do some talking.'

And they did talk, over coffee at a small round table in the kitchen. 'You've raised Cain,' Storm said as the old woman fussed around, pouring coffee for everyone.

'Yes, I know it. Sheila used to give me daily reports on what was happening in town. We thought until the last that they'd have to cut Nate loose — they having no proof that I was even dead, let alone that he had done it.'

'The jury's decision wasn't based on logic, Janet, it was anger and fear that prompted it. They wanted revenge on someone after the bank was robbed. They were angry and needed to find a target for that anger. You should have realized that it was time to come forward. Why didn't you?'

'I couldn't let my father go to prison,

Mr Hiller!' she said. She then buried her face in her hands. 'He's not young anymore. And my testimony would have been what sent him there to end his days behind bars.'

'You know for a fact that he's guilty of robbing his own bank?' Storm asked and Janet Teasdale lifted her tear-streaked face again.

She nodded miserably. 'I know it, yes.'

'But you chose to trade Nate Lydell's life for your father's freedom?'

'Oh, it wasn't that way at all. You don't understand. It was just the way it happened. I had to run away, and Nate knew that and agreed with me. You see, Mr Hiller,' Janet said, straightening and taking a deep breath, 'on the night of the bank robbery, I looked out the window and saw Father's favourite horse showing signs of being ridden hard, standing at the hitch rail. Two other horses — not ours — were also hitched there. Father was returning from the barn with a fresh horse.

'I decided to ask about it since I knew he was supposed to be down in Sexton at some sort of convention. I wondered why he had come back early.'

Storm only nodded. He thought they all knew why Teasdale had come back now. Riding through the night hard enough to have lathered his horse, then switching mounts for the ride back to Sexton. Oh, all of those solid citizens had seen him there, providing a tight alibi — the thing was no one could have seen him overnight when he made his desperate run to King's Creek and back. A man on a fast horse can cover a lot of ground in eight or ten hours — if the reason to do so is strong enough.

'It was still the middle of the night,' Janet Teasdale was saying, 'and Father had no business being home or sitting up at the kitchen table, but when I sneaked down the dark hallway that's where I found him. There were two other men with him so I kept away, being in my night gown.'

'Who were they?' Storm asked.

'One was Buck Dewar, our local copper company boss. I knew him because he and Father have talked many times in our parlour, usually with Mr Dewar trying to get yet another loan from the bank for his mining ventures.'

'Dewar wasn't doing that well, then?'

'Oh, he seemed to be on the surface,' Janet said as if it were a matter of indifference to her, 'but he had what they call a lot of 'cash flow' problems. He was proceeding on a grand scale as if the mines were inexhaustible — that's just what I overheard from time to time, you understand.' She shrugged.

'Of course, but Dewar was having some sort of financial trouble?' Storm asked.

'Some sort of quite large trouble,' Janet told them. There was still a low fire flickering in the hearth and it showed Janet Teasdale's concerned young face as she turned fully toward Storm Hiller and said, 'It was the other man with them that sent a chill up my spine.' She seemed to shudder at the memory. 'He was narrow and tall — I could tell that even when he was seated at the table. He had dark, almost lifeless eyes and a mouth that was quite wide but seemed almost fleshless, like a scar cut across his face. I don't know how else to describe him.'

'Handy Cooper,' Storm said. 'He was seen with them earlier at the bank, and the description sounds like him. He handles all of Dewar's rough work at the mine. It figures they would want him along, not knowing what problems they might run into.'

'What happened then?' Clara asked. She liked a good story. She was leaning forward from the stuffed white chair she was seated on, her hands clasped together, her eyes bright, eager.

'Then?' Janet's face was briefly reflective. It seemed she was struggling with her conscience. Still reluctant to break her silence, she finally told them, 'They had the sacks of money from the bank and they were counting out each man's share.'

'So you . . . ?'

'What was I to do, walk in and let them see that I had been hiding there? I'm not sure, but I thought the dark-eyed man might have seen me in the shadows. He was facing my direction, but he said nothing. I stayed up the rest of the night, until finally the three left. I heard my father say that they were going to have to make tracks to get back to Sexton before sun-up.

'I was up until dawn, then I dressed and rode over to Corkscrew. I had to talk to someone, and Nathan was the only one I trusted. He advised me to get as far away from the house as I could and stay as long as possible, keeping quiet about what I had seen.' Janet had started to cry softly, pitiably. 'And so I did just that, leaving Nate to the hangman.'

'Even having him go to trial for your murder didn't bring you forward,' Storm said. 'Why?'

'Well, the whole thing seemed farcical when it began — how could they convict him of murder when I was very much alive?' Janet hesitated, looking toward the low-burning fire. 'And if I told them why I had run away, I would have to tell them what I knew of the bank robbery. They would have sentenced my father to prison for the rest of his life.'

'The whole town needs your help now, Janet, and Nate is still waiting to be hanged. All of King's Creek is in turmoil — men are being killed all up and down the street.'

'I never meant for any of it to happen!' Janet Teasdale said. 'I was just looking for a way to avoid testifying against my father. I always believed Oretheon Bean would eventually solve this robbery, but I wasn't going to help him.'

As he likely would have. There were too many loose strings. The fact was absolutely beyond dispute that Patrick Teasdale was the only one who could have opened the safe. With enough poking around, Oretheon would have found a stable keeper, a single citizen of Sexton who had been up early and seen the bank robbers returning to town on well-used horses. Being thorough, Oretheon might have had someone ride the distance to Sexton at a hard gallop and prove that Teasdale could have come and gone in the ten hours or so he had had to work with.

'Time is up, Janet,' Storm said, rising to his feet. 'You had a plan but it didn't work. Your father did the crime and now he'll have to face up to it. All of King's Creek has need of you now if it is to survive — and that includes Nate Lydell, who is surely doomed one way or another if you don't appear.'

It didn't take nearly as long as Storm Hiller had feared to make up Janet Teasdale's mind and get her outfitted and ready for the night ride back to town.

The women were silent for the most part along the trail, but riding together as if for mutual support. It was Storm who set the urgent pace. When he had left King's Creek, hell had already broken loose, and they had passed the in-riding Corkscrew cowboys along the trail. These men would be primed for action, knowing that Marshal Bean held their boss and his son in jail, unable to fight or flee as the Belvedere crowd stormed the place, a wild-eyed mob with a gun in one hand and a rope in the other.

* * *

The far out-manned Oretheon Bean was trapped there as well, and what of poor Taffy? Had Bobby even been able to persuade the doctor to brave the hellish streets to visit the wounded deputy who seemed at death's door?

Within a mile they could again hear the sounds of gunfire, the remote 'pop' of weapons making no more noise, seeming to have no more destructive power than a child's firecracker. But there were dozens of fully armed citizens ahead and with every pop came

167

the possibility of a man's death.

Storm had drawn up on the rim of the hills, overlooking the besieged town of King's Creek. There was a small fire burning in one of the establishments below — the Golden Concubine Saloon, Storm thought, and muzzle flashes like sparks at this distance, flickered from virtually one end of the street to the other, from balconies, upstairs windows, in the streets and alleys below. Zebulon's Famous Restaurant, he noted, was dark and shuttered. Rube Yates's instinct for survival was a strong and useful one.

'Well,' Clara Fine said, sitting her dun pony beside Storm, 'we're here — now what are we going to do?'

Storm had already decided on his course of action, but he was uncertain as to its effectiveness. 'I'm going to try to get through their lines and reach the jail to talk to Oretheon.'

'Then?' Clara asked hopefully, doubtfully.

'I'll meet with the marshal and try to

convince him to show the white flag. Here's my thinking — when Randy Travis and his bunch see the flag, they will think that they've beaten him and that Oretheon is ready to hand over Nate Lydell to them. The Corkscrew boys might interpret a white flag as a sign that Bean has given up to protect himself and his town, and decided to surrender Jocko and his Nate to the cowboys for their protection.'

'That's a lot of supposing,' Clara said dryly. 'How do you know what any of them will do?'

'I don't, Miss Bacon,' Storm said in a rebellious student sort of voice, 'but it should at least cause enough of a break in the battle that you and Janet can make your way to the centre of the town safely and convince everyone that you are alive and all of this shooting is for nothing. That's what I hope,' he concluded, with fingers mentally crossed. 'Unless you have a better idea?' This last was said almost challengingly.

'I can't see why it shouldn't work,'

Janet Teasdale put in quickly, sensing the tension between the two which was simple to see but difficult to define. 'If all hands would only put their guns down for five minutes — I think this can be settled before more men are shot.'

'All right,' Storm said, 'I'll make my way to the jail and try to talk Bean into going along with my plan. If that can be done, there should be a cessation of the battle while Bean tries to pacify the leaders. That silence will be your signal to come forward.'

'What if you can't get to the jail, Storm?' Clara asked, now sounding worried. 'What if you can't get past those guns?'

'In that case,' Storm said with a stony expression on his usually amiable face, 'the plan is a bust, and you two might as well turn your ponies and head back to Gretel's cabin.'

'But you . . . ' Clara said in a near whisper.

'If I don't make it, I won't care

anymore, Clara. I'll be in a place where I just won't care about all of the world's small troubles.'

He turned his horse's head, offered Clara a smile, and started off down the hill toward the rage-infested town.

'He's a brave man, Clara,' Janet Teasdale said as they watched him go.

'Yes,' Clara agreed, her eyes still on Storm's back as he rode on alone into the firestorm that was King's Creek.

'He certainly has a nice smile.'

'He does,' Clara said with a nod. Janet sat watching her friend. Her horse blew impatiently, perhaps wanting to follow the black one along.

Janet Teasdale reached out and touched her friend's arm. 'Do you like him, Clara? Quite a lot?'

Clara's response began in a scoffing tone, 'With the occupation he has?' It ended with a whispered admission. 'Yes.'

★ ★ ★

171

The crack of rifle fire, the duller whump of handgun reports filled the night with muffled thunder. Every direction Storm glanced, gun muzzle fire flashed in the darkness. He had already passed the crumpled forms of two cowboys, unmoving against the cold earth. This had to be stopped! How did Patrick Teasdale feel about things on this night, or did the banker even realize that he had triggered it all with his greed? Would he even care?

There was no safe way to approach the jail. Certainly not from the street where pickets on either side blindly fired at every moving shadow in the other direction. It seemed that they had all brought plenty of ammunition and were determined to burn it up.

Trying to slip through the alleys would be equally treacherous. These would be guarded as well.

'Up and over,' Storm told his not understanding, uncaring horse. At the far eastern end of Main Street, he entered the narrow alley behind Slade

& Rafferty's trading post. That had been one of the first buildings in King's Creek, a low, solid, old log structure. He drew the horse up to the far side of the building, and had it stand while he climbed up to plant his boots on the saddle's curved back.

The horse began to move nervously as another volley of shots, much nearer, sounded. It didn't matter at all to Storm Hiller, who had already gotten his grip on the eaves and pulled himself up and over on to the roof.

The roof was mossy, dust-covered, the logs underfoot shedding bark. That made no difference to Storm either. It took him a dozen long strides to reach the opposite end of the roof, crouch and leap across the side alley to the Montrose Stable's roof. Below him a horse nickered, another answered, but Storm had already departed. To the end of the stable roof and across another narrow alley to the Harlequin Gaming House, quickly over that and to the saddlery where he landed roughly in an awkward leap, and had his breath briefly forced from him.

Storm had been intent on his gymnastics but not attentive enough to his surroundings. Ahead now, no more than twenty feet away he saw a man with a rifle kneeling, his sights on the jail house. Startled eyes turned toward Storm, and a shaggy, bearded man challenged him in the darkness.

'Who the hell are you?' the bearded man demanded. It was still the dark of night so Storm got away with his answer, gaining him the few extra seconds he needed.

'Why, it's me!' Storm called out, keeping his voice merry.

'Who . . . ? I don't know you,' the would-be sniper replied, and he swung his rifle muzzle in Storm's direction.

Storm's Colt was drawn, the hammer wheeled back, now he triggered off the .44 bucking in his hand as he shot the man. The rifleman swatted at his chest, tried to rise and turn at once and then rolled to his side, tumbling from the roof to the alley below to land with a thud which was barely audible with the constant roar of night-shouts, commands and gunfire around them.

Coiling himself for a running start, Storm leaped across the wider alley and hit the roof of the jail house. He rose rapidly — there was too much gunfire in this direction to suit him — and made his way to the edge of the roof overhanging the dynamite-damaged jail cell. Going to his belly he inched forward, wary of making an unannounced entry.

He lay there in the bloody cold of the night, listening to the gunfire below and beyond. Out in the street a man screamed horribly and yelled, 'They got me, Eddie!' which was likely the last thing he would ever say. Storm knew that he had to put a stop to this.

He hesitated to simply swing over and down into the gutted jail cell — a nervous friend could kill as easily as an enemy, and no one could know that Storm was there.

Listening to the rifle fire in the jail below and feeling the matching vibrations, he decided that there were two men firing from the front windows. Why had they abandoned the crumbled jail cell's defence? Oretheon and Bobby were protecting the street side of the jail only. Maybe they were counting on the attackers not realizing there was a breach in their defences.

He had to end this! To bring about just a five minute cease-fire when Janet Teasdale could come forward and tell them all that she was not dead, that there was no cause for Nate Lydell to be locked up, no cause to hang him.

It was a hasty and desperate decision, but Storm turned, found his grip and swung down into the dynamited cell underneath him . . .

. . . to face the Winchester gripped by Jocko Lydell. 'Welcome home, hangman,' Lydell growled.

Storm's heart sank. All of his efforts had ended, only in giving Jocko Lydell a second chance to kill him.

10

The abrupt silence amid the constant bedlam surrounding the jail house caught Marshal Bean's ear as surely as a sudden bang catches that of a man sitting in silence.

'What is it, Lydell?' he called out in a strained voice. 'Out of ammunition?'

'No, sir, I've got reinforcements for all the good he'll do us.'

'What are you saying?'

By the time Storm had entered the office, the marshal was up from his kneeling position. His face went through a series of changing expressions, ending with a broad smile. 'Well, I'm damned! How did you ever get back here, Storm? Come to think of it, where have you been for so long?'

Lydell returned to the cell; Bobby Ryder glanced up to only nod a welcome as he fired intermittently at outside targets.

'I'll tell you,' Storm said, letting the marshal return to his firing spot which seemed of more immediate importance to him at the moment. 'Tell me this, have you got a white flag we can hang out the window?'

'A what?' The look Bean shot Storm Hiller in response was many things, defiance chief among them.

'Let me tell you what's happened and what I'm thinking,' Storm said, taking an office chair and seating himself rather than joining in the on-going warfare. He began talking without Bean seeming to hear, but by the time he had gotten to the middle of his planned speech, Bean seemed as alert and eager as a hunting dog who's spotted its prey.

'By God,' Oretheon said emphatically, 'it's a chance, isn't it? A pretty good chance. If we show those men a good enough reason to stop shooting, prove to them that they've been foolish to embark on this war, they'll have to listen. We'll be giving enough proof that they will have to lay down their guns and go home, feeling only a little foolish instead of shot up.'

From the window where he knelt, Bobby Ryder glanced their way. 'You've seen Janet Teasdale in person?' he asked, needing to be cautious. 'And she's all right?'

'Not more than half an hour ago. She was fine then.'

From the back cell Nate Lydell called out wildly, 'Is Janet here? Did I hear you say that?'

'Not yet, but if what Storm says is true, I've no doubt she will be shortly. Jocko! Bring me a sheet off one of those bunks in there!' Bean himself went to the wall where the stars and stripes hung from a mounted staff. As he was removing the red and blue flag carefully, an uncertain Jocko Lydell came out of the ruined cell with one of the bed sheets.

So equipped, Oretheon opened the front door of the jail with ultimate caution, thrusting the white flag into the smoky night. It drew one bullet in

179

response, but the shooter seemed to be calmed by wiser heads and gradually the streets of King's Creek fell to uneasy silence.

They stepped out cautiously into the night of the jackals. Gun smoke filled the air, misting the stars. There was an anxious, uneasy mood in the streets. Storm could almost feel the eagerness of the men to return to what they understood best — gunfire.

'Ready to give it up, are you, Marshal? It's about time!'

Other voices shouted orders at each other. Finally, Randy Travis's distinctive raspy voice called out, 'Come on out of there, and bring your prisoner'

'Corkscrew!' Marshal Bean called out. 'Are you boys going to hold your fire?'

'They'll hold it,' Jocko Lydell assured Bean.

Lydell was in on the plan now and knew it could only lead to good for his son. Bean hollered to the Corkscrew riders, 'Fox, Charlie, this is Jocko

Lydell — mind the truce!'

The night became utterly still; gun smoke still floated through the air, clouding the faces of the few lighted buildings.

'All right, we're coming forward now,' Oretheon yelled and with a deep breath and a hopeful glance at Storm Hiller, he started out on to the jail house's porch, holding the flag of truce before him.

Storm had been surveying the far side of the street; now he saw what he had been hoping for and nudged Bean along, instructing him, 'Middle of the street, Oretheon.'

It was not a comfortable moment for any of the four men who now made their way forward. Not with rifles all around them. Bobby Ryder took a few shouted gibes which were hurled at him from the Corkscrew side.

'Who you riding for now, Bobby?'

'Which side are you on, Ryder?'

Bobby ignored the taunts, Jocko Lydell shot a hard look in the direction of the men who had yelled.

'Where's the kid?' Randy Travis shouted angrily. He was standing at the head of the mob, separated from them by some small distance. Beside him stood the stone-eyed gunman, Handy Cooper, his gaze boring into Storm Hiller. Oh yes, he knew Storm by now, remembered who had sent him to prison the last time.

'We didn't bring Nate out,' Oretheon said. There was a slight quaver in the marshal's voice; Storm thought that no one else could detect it, but it was there. He couldn't blame Bean — this was a deadly game.

'We didn't think we'd need him,' Storm said before he could be shouted down.

'You could get what you give, hangman!' Randy Travis said to a chorus of mumbled agreement.

'We brought her instead!' Storm shouted out, motioning to the opposite side of the street where a small, shy woman eased out into the bloody street accompanied by Clara Fine. The sudden, remarkable appearance of the redheaded woman already assumed dead startled the mobs to silence. To those who didn't recognize the young woman, men shouted, 'It's Janet Teasdale! Damn me, it's the dead girl!'

There were a dozen things Storm could think of shouting at Randy Travis, but he was silent, keeping his eye on Handy Cooper who still had reason for fear and anger. Cooper knew that the girl might have seen him at Teasdale's house on the night of the bank robbery — Janet had told them as much.

The more general reaction among the gathered fighters was shame. Storm saw a few men exchanging glances which admitted they had been fools for taking up arms against the town marshal, taking the word of Randy Travis as gospel.

Janet, looking as stunned and frail as ever, stood as close as she could to Clara Fine who also looked fearful, but challenged the crowd with her eyes.

A man in the front ranks of the Belvedere Mob said to Oretheon Bean, 'I guess we were wrong, Marshal, completely wrong. We meant to do the right thing . . . we'll see that the mess is cleaned up.'

'We can talk about all that tomorrow. For now, you boys owe your dead friends a funeral — and an apology.'

Storm's eyes were still fixed on Handy Cooper, who had twitched his thin lips and begun to reach for his gun. Handy was in a bind again, headed back to prison, and he knew it. He did not mean to go easy. Storm was not unprepared for Cooper's desperate move. Crouching, he had drawn his own .44, and as Handy's bullet spun over his head, shattering the silent congress, Storm fired in return. His first bullet took Handy Cooper in the leg, the second thudded into his chest and stopped his habit of living.

Randy Travis, apparently panicked, was caught up in things and he too slapped at his holstered sidearm. Oretheon Bean shot him dead.

Almost regretfully, Bean said as he holstered his weapon, 'I tried to warn that boy a dozen times, but he just kept making one mistake after the other.'

The remainder of the mob scattered, some with regret, some with a fear that they might be arrested for this night's work. A good share of them headed back toward the Belvedere Saloon which had remained open for business even in the middle of the war. Jocko Lydell was now shouting a few choice words at his Corkscrew riders, ordering them back to the ranch.

'Cows can't mind themselves!' they heard him bellow at some unlucky Corkscrew hands.

The street was nearly empty — there would have been no point in anyone but the dead lingering.

'I guess you'll be wanting to talk to me,' Janet Teasdale said to Marshal Bean. Her teeth were chattering either with cold or fear.

'You bet I will, Miss Teasdale, but the morning is soon enough. I'm tired and I'm hungry.'

'You can stay with me tonight,' Clara offered Janet, who smiled gratefully, but there was concern in her eyes. 'You'll be safe enough there,' Clara assured her.

'She sure will.' Nathan Lydell stood on the porch in front of the jail. He was buckling on his own gun belt. 'I'll sit up all night, if need be — I have had plenty of sleep lately. Hope you don't mind, Marshal. I looked around and found my gun in your desk.'

'Nate!' Jocko Lydell looked at his son as if he, too, had risen from the grave. There was the dull glint of tears in the old cattleman's eyes.

'I'll be needing another day or two off, Dad, but I'll be home as soon as I can.'

Before the elder Lydell could form an answer, Nate had stepped down from the porch and walked directly to Janet Teasdale, taking her into his arms. They started away toward Clara's rooms.

186

Storm asked, 'Do you want me to come along, too?'

'No,' Clara Fine said sharply, 'I don't think anyone will be needing you tonight, Storm.'

When Storm turned back, Oretheon Bean had a ragged smile on his face. 'Looks like you might as well stay at my house for another night, Storm.'

'I suppose so,' Storm answered heavily as they walked back to the jail, Bean's arm draped over his shoulders. 'How do you suppose Nate got out of his cell?'

'Guess someone forgot to lock it after I let Jocko out.'

'Good thing they did. Things worked out all right, but if they hadn't, Nate would at least have had a chance at slipping out the back and out-running the lynch mob.'

'I never thought of that,' Oretheon Bean said, looking away at the silent street. Storm smiled and patted the marshal's back.

'How's Taffy?' Storm asked.

'The doctor wasn't here long and didn't do much — he said he couldn't under the circumstances, but he set the leg roughly and provided me with a few packets of pain-reliever to give Taffy in the meantime.' Bean paused. 'I doubt he'll ever be able to return to work — too bad, he was a good man.'

They had not even been thinking about Jocko Lydell — maybe they had both put him out of their minds when the Corkscrew gang rode out. Now, the Corkscrew boss barked out, 'Come on, Bobby, let's get riding!'

Bobby Ryder, standing by the gun rack, turned his eyes on the Corkscrew owner. 'I thought I might be staying around here for a while,' he told him.

'What do you mean? What for?'

'Well, Marshal Bean don't have a deputy now,' Bobby said with his eyes turned down. 'I thought that if he was intending to hire another one, I might as well be first in line to apply for the job.'

Jocko Lydell's facial muscles bunched

themselves 'What are you talking about, Bobby? You're a cowboy first, last and —'

'Maybe not always,' Bobby Ryder interrupted, holding up a palm. 'If the marshal here will have me, I wouldn't mind trying my hand at peace-keeping.'

'You're crazy to think of leaving a life-time job with Corkscrew,' Jocko Lydell said. 'Especially when you don't even know if Bean will have you.'

'I'd like to at least try out Bobby,' the marshal said, settling finally into his swivel chair. 'He's shown me that if nothing else, he will stand his ground in a fight.'

'There's more to the job than that!' Jocko said, his eyes raking Bobby Ryder.

'Yes, there is,' Bean agreed, 'but all of that can be learned; nerve can't.'

Watching Bobby's face throughout the exchange of words. Storm thought he knew what was running through the cowboy's mind. Clara Fine had told him, and Sheila Porter felt the same — cowboys who were going nowhere, and hangmen were low on the list of men they would consider having. Bobby Ryder was trying to change the way he earned a living. Whether it would work or not remained to be seen, but he was changing his ways for Peony Cowper.

'All right then,' Jocko said, turning toward the door with his recovered hat and rifle, 'damn you, then!' His expression softened. 'And good luck, Bobby.'

* * *

Morning, when Storm awoke to it, was pleasant, bright and clear. No smoke lingered to smudge the blue skies, and no scent of gunpowder hung in the air. Storm felt sore and stiff. He had spent the previous day in long riding and violence. As a result, he was slow to awake on this morning, sleeping well past the cock's crow.

It took him a moment to even recall where he was and how he had come to be there. Slowly, he recognized Ore-theon Bean's bedroom, now slightly rearranged. Storm himself had dragged the bed to the far side of the room, well away from the small window. He had not been so tired the night before that he had forgotten about the shots fired through it at his last night in the place, Even though he knew that Randy Travis and Handy Cooper — the two men most likely to have done the shooting — were both beyond being able to attempt it again, a sort of primitive, protective impulse had caused him to place the bed out of harm's way.

He sat on the edge of the bed now and rubbed his head before reaching for his boots. This house, he reflected as he passed through it on the way to the back door, was not a bad little place — it was the sort a man could be comfortable in, if he had a woman to neaten it and welcome him home at night.

Oretheon Bean had never talked to Storm about his own wife who was gone now. Dead or departed, Storm did not know which. Maybe simply gone — a lawman's wife was not apt to have an easy life of it, either.

Storm recovered his black horse, which seemed in fine fettle on this bright morning, from the lean-to sized stable Bean had built, although Storm knew the marshal kept his own pony in the town stable.

Saddling, Storm started his horse toward King's Creek which lay just beyond the oak grove. It was an easy little jaunt, just enough for the horse to get the morning kinks out. Storm walked it along the fire-damaged street, noticing that three or four local men were out early, repairing the siding on a few of the buildings.

He glanced at Zebulon's as he passed the restaurant, his stomach urging him to stop for breakfast. Storm ignored that urging and the small tug at his heart which encouraged the same destination. He mentally slapped himself in the face.

Give that idea up, Storm. Clara Fine knew now that Storm was no hangman, but she probably sheltered the same prejudice against lawmen. Besides that, it was a fact that Storm had little more to offer a woman than some rambling cowhand. That is, he had a steady job all right, but one from which he might not return on any given day. All right then! He pushed thoughts of Clara Fine from his mind — or as far as they were willing to go.

Now approaching the jail, Storm saw a crew of men with shovels filling in the crater in the street where the dynamite had been ignited. He even recognized two of the men as Belvedere fighters from the night before. These glanced up at Storm and then turned their eyes quickly back to their work. They were ashamed of what they had done, and should be.

No other horses stood in front of the jail where Storm swung down to loosely hitch his own black one.

The office door was open — a rarity

these last few days. From within the jail house, Storm could catch the scent of the burned gunpowder lingering there. No wonder; when Storm had last visited the jail the night before, there were still clouds of gun smoke swirling in the air. Oretheon and Bobby had burned up a lot of ammunition in that confined space.

Storm stepped up on to the plank walk, made a show of scraping his boots, then rapped on the door frame before entering.

There was a large collection of glum faces in that room. Storm pasted on his best smile and greeted the assembled citizens of King's Creek. Eyes welcomed him with expressions from indifference to hostility.

Not a single one of them smiled back.

11

Marshal Oretheon Bean was there of course, seated behind his desk, wearing his hat. His face looked haggard, his eyes were pouched and red. He nodded to Storm.

'How're things out there?' he asked.

Storm realized that Bean had not had the chance to do his routine patrol of the streets for some time now, and it troubled the marshal.

'Looks quiet — and industrious,' he added with a smile.

Bobby Ryder was standing with a shined deputy marshal's badge pinned to what seemed to be a new yellow shirt. Near to him, but not too near, sat Sheila Porter which surprised Storm only a little. Maybe they had had some sort of swearing-in ceremony for Ryder earlier. The blonde woman looked a little proud, and a trifle protective.

Almost shrunken into the corner shadows was the bank teller, Colin Pierce, who stood, shifting from foot to foot nervously. Not far from him stood the two women: the main witness to events, Janet Teasdale, and the dark-haired little waitress . . . what was her name?

In the middle of the floor seated on a wooden chair, was the centre of attention, Mr Patrick Teasdale, his forehead glistening with perspiration despite the morning coolness.

'Get him out of here!' Teasdale thundered, laying eyes on Storm.

'No,' Oretheon answered calmly. 'You are in no position to give orders around here, Pat. Storm is an associated lawman assisting with the investigation.'

'What investigation?' Teasdale demanded. 'If you want, arrest me, give me my day in court! Charge me, or release me.'

Oretheon had his hands flat on his desk. His watery eyes levelled themselves on Patrick Teasdale's. 'In case you didn't understand me, Pat — you *have* been charged and arrested for the robbery of the King's Creek Bank.'

'Preposterous,' Teasdale scoffed unconvincingly. He turned enough in his chair to glance at his daughter who looked down and away.

'Not in the eyes of the law,' Oretheon said calmly. 'You'll have your trial — if that's what you demand. I brought you out this morning to give you the chance to plead guilty and save the court, as well as the others involved as witnesses, their time and money.'

Storm knew exactly what Oretheon Bean was doing; he was trying to avoid forcing Janet Teasdale to have to testify against her father in court. It didn't look like it was going to work; Teasdale was determined not to go down easy.

Oretheon went on. 'I'm sending Bobby Ryder — and Storm if he agrees to it — out to arrest Buck Dewar. Let's see what your accomplice has to say.'

Teasdale seemed to blanch a little at the mention of the mine boss, but he regained his composure quickly.

Before he could start an argument with Oretheon, Bean went ahead. 'If you insist on a court trial, of course we have to let you have it. Unfortunately, our third suspect will be unable to appear; he being good and dead. Randy Travis was killed in the middle of a commotion he himself raised.'

Teasdale seemed unaware of that, for his fixed expression altered just a little.

'Yes,' Oretheon went on, leaning back in his chair, hands behind his head, 'King's Creek, unfortunately, showed what it was made of when it thought Nate Lydell wasn't being hanged quickly enough to suit them. I wonder what they'd do if they took it into their heads that the man who had stolen their savings, hard-earned cash from the bank they had trusted . . . '

Oretheon's words trailed off. It didn't matter; he had never intended to finish the sentence.

Patrick Teasdale's face continued to hold defiance, but he seemed to be wavering just a little now. He stood, looked long at his daughter with what seemed to be a caring look, and was taken to his cell to think things over by Bobby Ryder.

'He'll do the right thing,' Clara said in a hopeful tone to the conscience-stricken girl who was the key witness in the matter of the bank robbery. Janet looked hopeful, doubtful.

'I just don't want to go to court,' Janet said. 'To testify against Father seems ungrateful, treacherous.'

'He'll come through — he's enough of a man,' Oretheon Bean said, standing behind his desk.

He was thinking that finding the loot from the bank would strengthen his case greatly. He had not yet had the time to search the banker's house or ride to Sexton to look for possible witnesses to Teasdale's night ride. From the back of the jail house a thin, reedy voice lifted.

'When am I going to get something to eat? Are you trying to starve me on top of everything else?'

Marshal Bean grinned. 'Someone better go get Taffy some breakfast.'

'Can't be done,' Storm Hiller said, tipping his hat back. 'Rube is fresh out of waitresses this morning.' He glanced at the two women in the room.

'Maybe for longer than that,' they heard Bobby Ryder mutter, then more loudly, 'I haven't eaten yet myself. Come along, Storm — with four of us there we should be able to get Taffy's grub for him.'

Storm hesitated. Clara took his arm, surprising him. 'Bobby's right — come on, Storm. Sheila and I have already left Rube in a bind this morning.'

'What about going after Buck Dewar?' Storm said, glancing at Oretheon Bean.

'It's a long ride to the mine,' Bean said, 'so no sense starting out hungry. This'll give you and Bobby a chance to discuss how you wish to handle it over breakfast.'

They made their way toward Zebulon's as an odd little parade. Bobby Ryder and Sheila walked in the middle, their arms interlaced. Storm was beside Bobby, Clara beside Sheila. Janet Teasdale had insisted that she could not eat so much as a bite this morning. Storm, at least, believed her. He had had emotions defeat appetite not once, but many times before. No amount of encouragement moved her so they left the banker's daughter in Oretheon's care for the time being.

Zebulon's was fairly quiet this morning. Many of the townspeople were still unwilling to show their faces, and Storm knew that Jocko Lydell would not be in the mood to grant extra privileges to any Corkscrew riders just yet.

They found a scattered crowd at the round tables, mostly shop keepers, a couple of teamsters from the freight office, and a forlorn-looking Nate Lydell, occupying a table by himself, turning an empty cup in his hands.

'Somebody'd better talk to him,' Bobby Ryder said, and Storm took it upon himself to do so.

Approaching Nate's table, he saw the kid's haunted eyes look up to him. Smiling, Storm swung out a chair, turned it and sat watching Nate Lydell for a minute.

Finally Storm said, 'You're a help, aren't you, Nate?'

'What do you mean?' Nate mumbled.

'Tell me, Nate, why'd you go through all of that — the trial and imprisonment?'

'You know why!' Nate flared. 'It was all for Janet.'

'Yes — this is a fine time to quit on her, isn't it?'

'I haven't — ' Nate began hotly. Storm cut him off.

'That's the way it looks to me, to everyone. Why aren't you with her now? She still needs you.'

'I didn't want to be there when she was forced to accuse her father. I know she would have cried, and to see her unhappy again would break my heart.'

'She hasn't had to testify against him yet, and Oretheon Bean has it fixed so that she may not ever have to. I know one thing, though; she won't get through this by herself, Nate. It takes more strength than the girl has. She needs you with her. Be a man and lend her some of your strength.'

'To go back into that jail again — '

'That's where Janet is,' Storm said, interrupting again. 'If you want her and you mean to stand with her from here on, don't sit here with your head hanging. Go over there with your spurs jingling! That's what Janet would expect of you.'

Nate sat there mutely, staring into his empty coffee cup. Storm rose, turned his chair and went to find the others who were now seated at the back of the restaurant. Clara's eyes were inquisitive.

'Well?' she asked.

'I don't know,' Storm, said. 'It seems that his time in jail has taken a lot out of him.'

Storm sat beside Clara — the only seat they had left for him, and glanced toward Nate Lydell. Within a minute the kid rose, put on his hat, and, his face set with determination, he walked out of Zebulon's, angling across the street toward the King's Creek Marshal's office.

Storm smiled. 'It seems I missed my calling. I should have been a preacher.'

'No,' Clara Fine said in a muted voice. 'No, you shouldn't have, but as long as you preached well enough to that young man this morning, you've done your share of good,'

''Morning Fiona, Miss Peony, gentlemen,' a tired-looking, faded woman of middle years said, approaching the table.

'We're done with that business with the names,' Sheila told her.

'Well, I was wondering when I saw you with . . . ' Her eyes swept over Storm and Bobby Ryder, both of whom were wearing their badges. 'What can I get for you, folks?'

'You can start with about a quart of coffee for me,' Bobby said. 'I don't know after that.'

'We'd better not eat now,' Clara said to Sheila. 'Rube is back there, waiting to scold us good and proper. Then we need to go to work.'

'Not for much longer,' Bobby Ryder said, sharing a lovers' look with Sheila Porter.

The waitress left the table and Storm asked, 'Who was that?'

'Her name's Delta Fox,' Clara said. 'She does the dishes and sometimes helps Rube with the cooking.'

'What's her real name?' Storm asked with a smile.

'That's it,' Clara answered. 'Honestly, Storm, you're incurably suspicious.'

'No, I wouldn't say so. It's that you two have me wondering if I'll ever take any woman in my life at face value again.'

'I wouldn't!' Sheila Porter said with a laugh. 'We're a conniving bunch.'

Clara and Sheila rose from the table and went to accept their deserved scolding from Rube Yates. Bobby Ryder's eyes followed the blonde until the two were well beyond his line of vision.

Delta Fox had returned with a pot of coffee and two cups for the men.

'Finally have her nailed, do you?' Storm commented after Delta had gone.

'I'm not positive of that, and it's making me nervous. Nothing is sure until the preacher ties the knot, is it? Girls have been known to back out before now.'

'That's true,' Storm said, sipping at the black, strong coffee. 'Sheila doesn't mind that you're a lawman?'

'No, she doesn't. As a matter of fact, it's the one thing that helped me to convince her. You know that Marshal Bean has a city-provided house?' Storm nodded. 'I've never seen it, but the marshal said that we could have it for now. He said he's got a bunk and everything he needs in his office — or will after Taffy can be taken out of there — and he doesn't much like dusting and housework and can't cook anyway, so he doesn't really need the place.'

'That'll be handy,' Storm said. 'I've

been in the house, it's a nice enough place.' Except that it needed new glass in one of the windows.

Storm was given pause to wonder. Did Bean really prefer staying in the jail house, or was the house an exceedingly generous wedding present? Only Bean could know that, of course, or needed to.

Bobby asked, 'What sort of living accommodations does a deputy sheriff have down in Raton?'

He was asking for more than one reason. His eyes flickered toward Clara Fine as she crossed the room, carrying a tray to a front table, then returned his gaze to Storm Hiller. Storm took a swallow of coffee, crossed his forearms on the table top and said, 'Now, this Buck Dewar — I assume you must have been out to his mine at one time or other. Does he have a house as well; will we be able to take him unaware?'

Clara Fine was crossing the restaurant on her way back to the kitchen. She smiled brightly and glanced at the back table, but all she saw were two men intensely discussing their job for the day, which she knew was a dangerous one, judging by what little she had heard. Frowning as she returned to the serving window, she exchanged a silent worry with Sheila Porter.

Minutes later, Storm Hiller and Bobby left the restaurant and within half an hour, they were riding toward the low red hills to the north of the town.

'The copper mine is open-pit,' Bobby Ryder said, continuing the conversation they had begun at the breakfast table. 'It's actually two mines: the Big Emma and the Little Emma, between these two pits is a cluster of shacks — the mine office, supply building and equipment shed.'

'You know a lot about it,' Storm said.

'Hell, you know how it is — on payday, the miners all drift into town and all they've got to do is drink and talk about their jobs. The cowboys are just as bad, I guess. Talking about things nobody else understands or cares about. A part of this stuck with me; it's bound to if you hear the same story fifty different times told fifty different ways.

'Now, as I see it, if Dewar hasn't already made his escape, he's most likely to use the — '

Storm suddenly reined up and shushed Bobby Ryder. 'I don't think we need to worry about any of that anymore,' he said, pointing ahead to where a two-passenger covered buggy could be seen down through the red sandstone bluffs toward the flats below.

'It's Buck Dewar!'

'Bound to be,' Storm answered, 'but who's that with him, handling the team?'

Bobby was either more familiar with the man than Storm was or had younger, sharper eyes. He told Storm, 'It's Bert Crayne driving.'

Storm only nodded. He was not discounting the big-shouldered Crayne, but at least they knew now that it was going to be two men against two and they would not have to face a number of mine workers who would rise up to fight any threat to their boss as readily as any cowhand fighting for the brand. Relief showed on the largely untested Bobby Ryder's face. He felt comfortable about his chances of bringing Buck Dewar in now with Storm Hiller at his side.

The two-horse team had emerged on to the red plain and was now making their way southward across flat prairie.

'How do you want to do this, Storm?'

'It's your arrest, Bobby, your jurisdiction. There's no county charge against the man. I'm only along for company.'

'Well . . . ' Bobby Ryder's face was dubious. It was obvious he hated to ask, but he recognized that Storm Hiller was an old hand at such problems. 'How would you stop these men?'

'What were you thinking of, Bobby?'

'I was thinking we could follow behind single file. They might not ever turn their heads to look back until they get to where they're going.'

'If they didn't, we might trail them all the way to Mexico,' Storm said. There was no mockery behind his smile, but obviously he had a better idea of how to halt the two runaway outlaws. Bobby asked Storm again what he had to recommend.

'You won't like it,' Storm replied, 'but it's only good sense. We have to shoot one of their horses — that will stop the buggy.'

Bobby frowned. 'You're right, I don't like it.'

'I don't, either, but it's the best way. Let's try and find a good place to ambush them.'

They started southward on a parallel course to the buggy. Bobby was trying to figure why Storm's plan bothered him. After all, if he saw a bank robber trying to escape on horse and he shot the animal from under him, he would feel no regrets. He forced himself to deal with the work at hand, which was enforcing the law by the best means available.

Two miles on, they came to a spot where the wagon track was squeezed between surrounding red hills, and the buggy would be forced to slow climb the grade. Their own horses were still fresh and exhibited no unwillingness to mount the low hills from that side. The buggy could still be seen to the north, following an arrow-straight line toward the spot where the lawmen meant to halt the bandits' run toward freedom.

Dismounting, Storm and Bobby edged up to the lip of the cut. The trail below was no more than a hundred feet deeper. It would be an easy shot.

'They'll start shooting as soon as the horse goes down,' Bobby Ryder said in a low voice as the plume of red dust from the buggy's wheels drew nearer.

'What are they going to shoot at? We're not showing ourselves. They might try to cut the dead animal out of its harness — no, they won't have time for that. If they decide to run, where is there to run to? No, Bobby, we've finished it here. We've left them with no choice but to surrender.'

They settled in behind a screen of sage and sumac, keeping themselves low. They could now hear the steady clopping of the horse team's hoofs. Storm heard an angry word thrown out by one of the men. It had been settled. Bobby Ryder was to shoot the nearest horse as they passed, Storm ready with his Winchester in case the men did take a notion to try shooting back. Storm thought that there would be no time in the first minute for the outlaws to even consider that. As the horse went down, the off horse would undoubtedly behave in panic, try to turn away or rear. The driver, Bert Crayne, would have his hands full trying to maintain control of the horse. That would leave the mine owner, Buck Dewar, to fight back, but Dewar would find no targets for his gun.

'When Bert climbs down to try to figure out how to cut the dead horse out of leather,' Storm told the young deputy marshal, ' that's the time to announce yourself and order their surrender.'

Bobby nodded; his throat was as dry as the desert and he only hoped some stern command didn't emerge as a squeak. Storm had been continually glancing northward, but there was no one following them from the mine. Dewar would have wanted no one else along, it would have meant splitting the stolen money further. No, the two men below were absolutely alone in this desolate canyon, which led nowhere at all except to jail or the grave.

12

It was another long minute in the canyon heat, conferring, before a cautious Bert Crayne stepped down from the buggy, his eyes searching the bluffs above him. Drawing his knife from a sheath hanging from the back of his belt, Crayne moved toward the downed horse, intending to cut the harness away. Buck Dewar could be seen beneath the buggy's unfolded top, holding a rifle grimly. Both men knew they were in a fix now if they did not act quickly. Storm and Bobby Ryder didn't intend to give them the time they needed.

Bobby and Storm stood watching each other. Suddenly taking resolve, Bobby gave his first order as the lawman in charge.

'We'd like to have Buck Dewar alive to testify, if possible. I don't think he'll fight, but who can tell with a desperate man? Bert Crayne we know will fight, but he's in a bad position to try much just now. Take Crayne, Storm; I'll try to slip up and disarm Dewar.'

'Right. If he raises that rifle in my direction, though, Bobby, I'd appreciate you taking any measures you have to to keep him from putting a hole in my body.'

Storm was smiling, but Bobby knew that the remark was quite serious. 'Our own protection comes first,' Bobby told him and with a nod, Storm swung into the saddle and guided his horse down the slope of the canyon wall toward the bank robbers.

There was no way men already on the alert could fail to hear the hoofs of the approaching horses. Storm saw Bert Crayne straighten up from his work with a start and begin to draw his gun. He tried to call out a warning.

'Throw down your weapon, Crayne, and ... ' That was as far as he got. Crayne was not in the mood to grow docile.

216

The town bully was heading for prison and a long stretch there, and he knew it. Maybe at that moment he regretted ever tying up with Buck Dewar for mere money. No matter what he was thinking, his actions spoke louder.

Bert Crayne never had a chance.

Probably Crayne had already known it as he rose from his crouch, slapping at his holster. Any lawman coming upon him that way would have his own weapon already levelled at the man he meant to arrest. Storm Hiller was no exception. He had his rifle at the ready and before Crayne could finish his half-spinning move and get a shot off, Storm had delivered a shocking message from the law with his Winchester. It was a dead shot. There were no theatrics; Crayne simply puddled up against the ground, dead. Storm heard Bobby Ryder yell out from the other side of the buggy.

'Lower that rifle, Dewar, and give it up if you want to live to see tomorrow!'

Within minutes, Bobby had the man down from the buggy, facing away from him with raised hands. Storm circled the buggy and leaned out to unlatch the small freight compartment at the back. He came up with a green canvas bag with the name of the King's Creek bank stencilled on it.

'That doesn't look like all that much,' Bobby Ryder said as Storm approached.

'We still haven't found Patrick Teasdale's cut,' Storm reminded him.

'You have any idea where to look for that?'

'First place I'd try is that bank in Sexton town. We know that the banker from Sexton was at the same meeting as Teasdale. Maybe — for a consideration — he would give Teasdale a place to stash the goods. A bank is the best place I can think of to hide money.'

'I wouldn't have thought of that,' Ryder said.

'It might not be much of a thought; it just occurred. Oretheon can probably find out pretty easily now that he's free to ride again. If Teasdale doesn't confess, the marshal will probably take the ride down there and back anyway, timing it, just to have a fact to put before a jury.'

'What about this one?' Bobby asked, nodding at the beaten Buck Dewar, who was standing with his hands up, leaning against the buggy, perspiration glossing his face in this hot, airless canyon pass.

'I doubt he'd know anything about that end of things,' Storm said. 'Can't see why Teasdale would share that sort of information with him. We'll let Oretheon handle the questioning on that, too. You'll be expected to hang around and listen, see how a marshal does these things.'

'I'd be pleased to,' Bobby Ryder said earnestly. 'I've got a lot to learn. But you, Storm, what are you going to do when we get back to town?'

'Get to bed early. This is my last night in King's Creek and the last night that the marshal's house will be available. You and Sheila will want to start looking the place over, moving furniture. Maybe painting it up.'

'I suppose,' Bobby said, looking as if it was only now coming home to him what he was in for, now that he had gotten what he wanted. 'If you're going by Zebulon's to eat, would you tell Sheila I'm all right?'

'I'm not going there,' Storm said firmly.

'No?' Bobby seemed surprised. 'I thought that you'd . . . '

'I don't expect to have much of an appetite,' Storm said. Both knew they were not talking about food.

'I don't know where you're going, or care — though I could make a suggestion about that!' a defeated looking Buck Dewar said angrily. 'Just get me somewhere out of the sun!'

'Might as well,' Storm said. 'I don't see any likely looking trees around here. We'll have to take you back to town to deal with.'

'Do you want to let him take the

buggy?' Bobby asked.

'No, it'd be hard to handle as it is. Cut out the live horse and he can ride back with us.'

'That's not a riding animal,' Dewar complained, 'and I haven't got a saddle.'

'Well, King's Creek isn't far, is it?' Storm said to the mine boss. Buck thought if he could, he would like to strangle the hangman, because — damn the man — he was smiling at him as he said that!

13

Storm Hiller watched as Bobby Ryder took a sun-beaten, angry Buck Dewar up on to the porch before the jail and in through the door. There was no need for Storm to go in. His part of the job was over; his time in King's Creek was done. He took the time to walk around to the rear yard of the jail, where the Platte cousins were found resting in the shade of the plank fence, each with a bottle of beer in hand. Their completed project, the exactly-made scaffold of green pine lumber stood as a testament to their endeavours.

Timmy Platte nudged his cousin with his elbow and both men watched with some trepidation as Storm made a show out of minutely inspecting the platform. Finished, Storm approached them, a broad smile on his face.

'A fine job, men! Just excellent. It's a

shame we no longer have a use for it.'
He shrugged. 'Oh well, it's bound to be
called upon one of these days. If you
haven't been paid yet, see the marshal
and tell him that I considered it one of
the finest scaffolds I've ever been
associated with.'

'Yes, sir,' Timmy answered with a
beaming smile. He was flushed with
pride. 'It's a shame you won't be able to
try her out yourself.'

'Yes, it is,' Storm agreed, 'but that's a
part of a hangman's woes.'

Leaving the self-satisfied carpenters
behind, he returned to the front of the
jail and unhitched his horse and the
surviving bay from the team the mine
boss had been using, and walked them
down the street to the stable.

Entering the high-ceilinged building,
he called out for a stable hand and then
whistled sharply, neither of which got
him a response but the interest of a lot
of horses waiting for their owners to
return.

Storm decided there was nothing for

it but to take matters into his own hands, so he led his horse and the bay along the aisle between the rows of stalls until he found two empty boxes, side by side.

Unsaddling his horse, he gave it a cursory rub down. There was still no stableman in evidence when Storm gave each horse a scoop of oats from the bin, took a last look around and walked to the door which was a bright rectangle in the brilliant sunlight. Squinting against the sun, Storm could make out the silhouetted figure of a man standing just outside, the stable hand at last — now that he had done the man's work for him.

That wasn't the case. There was something peculiar in the way the man held himself. Storm recognized the crooked figure just before the man spoke and brought up his revolver with his good arm.

'You killed me; now I'll kill you!'

Boy Coughlin's voice was a sort of strangled croak, but his Colt spoke very well, and Storm was jerked around as it sent a bullet slamming into his upper thigh. For reasons known only to him, Boy then holstered his pistol and turned to walk away, his chicken-wing arm flapping.

He didn't get far. From the marshal's office, Bobby Ryder came running, his own pistol held high. He threw down on Boy and ordered him to stop, and Boy Coughlin complied, looking confused as to what had happened, as if he had no memory of shooting Storm. Perhaps he did not.

Storm lay on his back just inside the stable door. Oretheon Bean had appeared to stand over him with two townsmen Storm had not met.

Oretheon ordered one of them roughly, 'Get the doctor! Now!' And the man scurried away. 'You're going to make it, Storm,' Bean added, squatting beside Hiller, his bulky shadow shutting out the glare of the day.

Storm nodded, smiled, and blacked out.

★ ★ ★

It was a lovely morning, the sky outside the window was blue with a few pearly clouds, only a gentle breeze ruffling the oak trees in the yard. He thought it couldn't be nicer even if he knew who he was, where he was and his leg didn't suddenly flare up with pain. It hadn't done that while he was asleep, why now?

The realization came to Storm Hiller — the resurgent pain had come, disturbing his sleep, awakening him to this strange world which slowly pieced itself together. In order, it came back to him: he was Storm Hiller, had been shot, and was lying in the bed in Marshal Bean's house.

'The doctor left some more powders in case the pain still needed relief.' The face of the girl was blurred, but her voice very familiar.

'What're you doing here, Clara?'

'I'm your nurse. The doctor said you should have a nurse around in case you decided to get up and get a drink of water, or go out chasing outlaws or something.'

'I'm not up to chasing outlaws,' he replied, 'but a glass of water doesn't sound half bad.'

Clara Fine nodded and went to the round table in the corner where a pitcher of water sat. She took one of the packets the doctor had left, sprinkled it into the water and stirred the concoction.

Storm took the water and drank it down. It had a bitter opiate taste. He laid his head back on the pillow.

'I thought Bobby Ryder and Sheila were going to take over this house.'

'They decided they did not need to move in immediately, not in the light of your greater need. I still have my rooms in town; they're staying there,' Clara said. She seated himself on the foot of the mattress.

'Did the doctor say how long I'll be laid up?' he asked, as a fresh twinge of pain shot through his leg.

'I don't think he knows for sure — not for long, he says.'

'So you've just stayed on here?'

'Yes — who else was there to do it?'

'Must get really boring,' Storm commented, closing his eyes as the pain now demanded.

'It hasn't been bad. Sheila comes by almost every day while Bobby is at work. We talk and do some of the cleaning up that's going to need doing when she and Bobby move in.' She stretched her arms, intertwining them overhead, yawning. She continued. 'The marshal has already taken the few things he wanted out of here. Now that Taffy is getting along better and has been moved out, Oretheon has all the room he needs or wants, he says.

'Janet has been by a few times. She's been living in the Teasdale house, as has Nate. It's close enough to Corkscrew that it's no problem him getting to work. They have been dividing their time between the two places. Jocko Lydell has always liked Janet. He likes the idea of having her as his daughter-in-law.'

'What's become of Patrick Teasdale?'

'He made a full confession. You were right about most of the stolen money having found its way to the Bank of Sexton.'

'What are they going to do with him?'

'A trial, of course, when the circuit judge arrives. Most folks seem to think that his confession and advanced years will mean a shorter sentence for him, but who knows? Having gotten their money back and maybe learned their lesson with Nate Lydell, at least no one in King's Creek is calling for a lynching.'

'That's progress, I suppose,' Storm said. His eyes were open again, just watching the slender brunette, who sat patiently watching over him. 'What became of our actual hanging victim, that little gnome who shot me?'

Clara smiled and patted his uninjured leg. 'Oretheon took his gun away and sent him home to sleep with the dogs. Boy Coughlin has no memory of shooting you. He got a little agitated when they told him that he had.'

'Short drop, for sure.'

'What?' Clara's eyebrows drew together. Storm shook his head; it didn't matter. She went on. 'Anyway, Oretheon let him go. They couldn't legally charge Boy with anything. Because legally Boy Coughlin is already dead. I didn't understand all that, but Oretheon said that you would.'

'It's true,' Storm said, hiding his own yawn. The opium the doctor had prescribed was starting to work now. 'When the territory hanged Boy Coughlin, his death sentence had been carried out — he was dead as of that moment. One day, we'll get someone clever in the capital chambers and he'll figure out the law has this large loophole in it and maybe they'll amend the way the law reads now.'

'It seems to me that Boy Coughlin is dead,' Clara said. 'Whatever dangerous gunman he once was, whatever he has done in the past, has been erased even from his own mind.'

'True. It seems the only man in the universe he hates is his hangman, and I had to appear that way.'

'The next time he sees you he's likely to say hi and want to shake your hand,' Clara said. 'He really only has that much of a memory.'

'I know; it's a pity what's been done to him. I suppose he deserved it — or rather the man who was once known as Boy Coughlin did.'

'You really do have pity for the man,' Clara said with surprise. 'Even after he shot you, I don't quite understand, Storm. Surely you've shot other men, killed a few in your time?'

'I have,' Storm had to admit, 'but this is the first one I've had come back to haunt me.' Something emerged from his clouded thoughts and he murmured, 'How are you getting all this time off?'

'That's simple,' Clara answered with a laugh. 'We quit — Sheila and me both. Rube was boiling mad. He said, 'I hope this town don't have any more available lawmen. I won't be able to keep my good help stocked!''

'You told Rube Yates that you were marrying me?'

'Oh, that?' Clara looked shyly away. 'He sort of came to that conclusion, Storm, seeing that I was with you day and night. I didn't say anything to contradict his thinking.'

Storm paused for a long minute. Just when Clara thought he had fallen to sleep, he said, 'Just make sure you give the preacher your right name, Fiona.'

He was smiling as he said it, and he dropped off to sleep with the smile still on his lips.

We do hope that you have enjoyed reading this large print book.

Did you know that all of our titles are available for purchase?

We publish a wide range of high quality large print books including:
**Romances, Mysteries, Classics
General Fiction
Non Fiction and Westerns**

Special interest titles available in large print are:
**The Little Oxford Dictionary
Music Book, Song Book
Hymn Book, Service Book**

Also available from us courtesy of Oxford University Press:
**Young Readers' Dictionary
(large print edition)
Young Readers' Thesaurus
(large print edition)**

For further information or a free brochure, please contact us at:
**Ulverscroft Large Print Books Ltd.,
The Green, Bradgate Road, Anstey,
Leicester, LE7 7FU, England.
Tel:** (00 44) 0116 236 4325
Fax: (00 44) 0116 234 0205

THE KILLING DAYS

Neil Hunter

Corruption is running rampant between members of government and powerful businessmen: bribery, conspiracy, and illegal dealings. Henry Quinlan, sent by Senator Howard Beauchamp to investigate, patiently compiled a dossier of evidence against the culprits. When he dispatched his documentation to the senator by train, protected by two Pinkerton detectives, it was stolen en route — and Quinlan disappeared. Now Jason Brand has been called in to track down both the dossier and its author. But someone's determined to stop him . . .